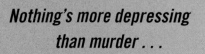

P9-DMT-124

*Nothing's more depressing
than murder . . .*

Also by Jill Churchill

Jill Churchill can be contacted at
Cozybooks@earthlink.net or through her website
www.JillChurchill.com.

JILL CHURCHILL

LOVE for SALE

AVON BOOKS

An Imprint of HarperCollinsPublishers

This is a work of fiction. Names, characters, places, and incidents are products of the author's imagination or are used fictitiously and are not to be construed as real. Any resemblance to actual events, locales, organizations, or persons, living or dead, is entirely coincidental.

AVON BOOKS
An Imprint of HarperCollins*Publishers*
10 East 53rd Street
New York, New York 10022-5299

Copyright © 2003 by The Janice Brooks Trust
Excerpt from *It Had to Be You* copyright © 2004 by The Janice Brooks Trust
ISBN: 0-06-103122-4
www.avonmystery.com

First Avon Books paperback printing: March 2004
First William Morrow hardcover printing: June 2003

Avon Trademark Reg. U.S. Pat. Off. and in Other Countries, Marca Registrada, Hecho en U.S.A.
HarperCollins® is a trademark of HarperCollins Publishers Inc.

Printed in the U.S.A.

10 9 8 7 6 5 4 3 2 1

LOVE for SALE

Chapter 1

Tuesday, November 1, 1932

It was late morning and the weather had suddenly turned cold. Lily Brewster and her brother, Robert, were sitting in the dining room of the mansion known as Grace and Favor, arguing over Governor Franklin Roosevelt and the upcoming election. It was a fairly amiable tiff.

"But what does he really mean by 'the New Deal,' and 'the Forgotten Man'? And why only men?" Lily asked. "Why not 'the Forgotten People'?"

"It's political rhetoric. But it sounds good. And the word 'the' before it means 'mankind.' "

"Why isn't he explaining, at least a little bit, what he means? It couldn't hurt him to be a tiny bit specific, could it?"

"Why should he tell President Hoover what he's going to do? Hoover might have enough brain cells left to get in and do it first. Lily, even if Roosevelt wins next week, which he certainly will, he can't do a thing until March. Which is so stupid."

"But won't he need some time to come up with a cabinet?"

"Not five months. There's already talk about moving the inauguration to early January. That would give an incoming president plenty of time. In fact, I'd bet Roosevelt already has his list ready right now. He's been in politics most of his life and has a huge circle of friends."

Robert was flipping through the latest issue of the *Voorburg-on-Hudson Times*. "I'm glad Mr. Prinney is no longer riding herd on Jack Summer. Young as he is, he's a good reporter. He's still dogging the Bonus March. According to his sources, Hoover said he would allow MacArthur and his toadies to use the Army to run the men out of Washington only if Superintendent of Police Pelham Glassford signed a statement that he was asking for the Army's help. MacArthur told the President that Glassford had done so.

"It was an outright lie," Robert went on. "Glassford hadn't even been asked to make such a request. Hoover should have busted MacArthur to private. Or pitched him out of the Army on his big fat head. But he did nothing."

"And does that surprise you?" Lily asked. "It's widely known MacArthur was forbidden to cross the Eleventh Street Bridge or use weapons. And MacArthur ignored the orders. Those pictures of the tanks crossing the bridge and Patton with his cavalry and swords drawn were horrifying."

Robert said, "But can't you just imagine MacArthur telling Hoover how the country was grateful to him, Hoover, for getting the commies out of the Capitol and Hoover believing it and taking the credit? That's why Governor Roosevelt is going to win the election. Hoover was wrong to take the credit for the traitorous acts of MacArthur. Whatever Roosevelt means to do, he means to do *something*. Hoover is a pushover.

"Putting the entire burden of the Depression on the Red Cross and private charities is ridiculous," Robert went on. "The Red Cross had already run out of supplies, and when they do have them, they don't know where they are. Banks are going down like ninepins. There's a drought in the breadbasket of the country, and farmers are losing their farms. So much for Hoover's statement about a chicken in every pot and a car in every garage. Not with Henry Ford shutting down his plants and laying off sixty thousand people. I don't care *what* Roosevelt does. It's necessary to simply do anything that puts people back to work and to get the crooked bankers in jail for putting their customers' money into the stock market."

"Okay, okay. You convinced me. But how do you think Governor Roosevelt is going to fix this?"

"Lily, you're not really paying attention. Roosevelt is the sort of man who tries things, and if they don't work, he tries something else that might. He's not a man who sticks to his guns when an idea fails. Hoover does nothing and pretends it works. I'm going to run down to Voorburg and talk to Jack Summer and see if he knows anything he's not printing in the paper."

"While you're there, would you pick up ten pounds of flour for Mrs. Prinney to make biscuits? She says the grocer has run out of yeast and doesn't know when he can get more. Hers died."

Robert looked puzzled. "Her what has died?"

"The yeast."

"Yeast is a living thing? Good Lord above. I'll never eat bread again."

"It's not still alive when you eat it. Are you going to give up all meat since it was once alive?"

Robert said, "I guess you have a point."

When he had gone, Lily was a bit at loose ends. She helped Mrs. Prinney in the kitchen for a while, but when the doorbell rang, she had to answer it because Mrs. Prinney was elbow-deep in a salad she was making for lunch and Mimi the maid was washing linens.

The man at the front door was wearing an enormously heavy, expensive-looking winter coat. His hat was pulled forward, and what little of his hair showed was obviously a cheap wig. His eyes were shaded with sunglasses.

"I'm James Smith. I understand you rent out rooms."

"We do sometimes. Would you like to come inside? I'm Lily Brewster."

Mr. Smith, if that was really his name, didn't remove his hat or glasses, but looked around. "I need to house three of my business associates and myself for a few days in privacy," he said.

"We have a large bedroom at the end of the second-floor hall that could serve as a meeting room, with attached bath and valet quarters. But your other people would have to stay in smallish rooms on the third floor. To give you a price, we'd need to know what meals you'd require and how long you're staying."

Lily was wary of him. She'd give him the highest price she could imagine to discourage him. But he beat her to the punch. Fishing in his coat pocket for a wallet and turning his back to her for a moment, he handed her ten fifty-dollar bills.

"Would this do for a down payment?" he asked. "Cost is irrelevant. Complete privacy is vital. We'd want to stay from Friday evening to Monday or Tuesday morning."

Lily pocketed the bills in the apron she was still wearing. "I can let you know later today. It isn't entirely up to me. Could you give me a telephone number to call and let you know?"

"No. I'll call you at eight this evening. Show me this room."

She took him upstairs and to what had once been Great-uncle Horatio's enormous bedroom, then Robert's room for a while until they had renovated it for special guests. She showed the visitor that there was also a small hallway that led to a bathroom and a servant's room.

Mr. Smith took a quick look around. "We'd need that bed moved out of the middle of the room and a worktable and chairs brought in to replace it. I'll let myself out."

She hurried to follow him, but he was surprisingly light on his feet. He darted out of the mansion and around the corner. She couldn't even get a glimpse of what sort of transportation he had. But even with the overly generous down payment, she was frightened of him.

He disappeared and she went back to the kitchen and told Mrs. Prinney about the visitor. "He was in a disguise, but let me show you what he gave me." She pulled out the money.

"Oh, my! What a lot of money!" the older woman exclaimed. "You're not going to turn him down, are you?"

"What if he's the leader of a bunch of gangsters?" Lily asked. "I read in the paper that Pretty Boy Floyd pays people or buys them booze to hide his gang. We don't know who this man is, and no amount of money would justify letting gangsters use the house."

"Did he look like a gangster?"

"I don't know." She described the way he was dressed and wigged and the bland name he'd given. "He could have been anyone. I couldn't even see enough of him to guess his age."

"You'll have to consult with Elgin and your brother. But it's a lot of money, dear."

"It is," Lily said, caressing the bills. "And it's only the down payment, he said. But I'm not sure we need it enough to have mysterious men in the house. What if they bring guns and rob a bank?"

"Voorburg doesn't have a bank anymore," Mrs. Prinney pointed out. "It went bankrupt before you even came here to live."

As did our father, Lily thought. She and Robert had grown up as spoiled rich kids until the Crash, when their father had mortgaged all their homes and invested everything in the stock market. Then jumped out the window of the broker's fifth-floor office.

The debate at dinner defeated Lily. "We're supposed to be earning our own living," Robert pointed out. "And if this is only part of what they'll pay, who cares who they are?"

Mr. Elgin Prinney, Esquire, was the executor of the Brewster's inheritance of their great-uncle Horatio's estate. Under the conditions of Horatio's will, the siblings had to live in Voorburg and support themselves for ten years, only being gone from Voorburg for two weeks total during each year. Mr. Prinney had moved his wife and himself into Grace and Favor to make sure Robert and Lily followed the rules. He had to be consulted about anything financial.

Mr. Prinney was on Robert's side. The elderly

and prissy lawyer said, "If they want complete privacy, it's to our advantage. What we don't know about their business can't hurt us, and we can't be held responsible. And they probably are quite respectable people who just want to work out something away from the prying eyes at their normal office. Lots of highly placed business executives can still afford to take their top people to out-of-the-way places to plan things. Takeovers and such."

Even Mrs. Prinney took up the theory. "Lily, I suspect you're letting your imagination run away with you. Maybe it's his real name. Maybe he's bald and wears a wig because he wants to look younger than he is. We wouldn't have to do anything with them but take up their meals to the big bedroom."

"Mrs. Prinney is right," Robert chimed in. "It's not as if we'd have to socialize with them and feed them in the dining room with us. I could get the Harbinger boys to dismantle one of the tables stored in the basement and take it up to the bedroom. They'd like to be paid to do it."

Only Phoebe Twinkle, the town milliner and seamstress who lived at the mansion as their boarder, was on Lily's side; however, she knew she had no real right to interfere and kept silent during the discussion. But she took Lily aside after dinner and said, "I think Robert or Mr. Prinney should take the food up. They shouldn't even see Mimi, Mrs. Prinney, or you or I."

"You think they're gangsters, too?"

"Not really. I think Mr. Prinney's right. They might even be politicians, planning something for this election. That's my theory. Maybe with the vote for President coming up, they're Hoover's men trying to come up with a frantic last-minute plan to get him in. Or, I hate to say it, but they might be Reds planning to disrupt the election."

She started upstairs to do some of her sewing, but stopped and added, "But the women in the house shouldn't be involved except maybe for the extra cooking."

"Are you worried about being on the same floor with the other men?" Lily asked.

"Not at all. The bedroom doors all have good locks, and so do the bathrooms. Put them all at the end that has the men's bathroom, though. It's farther from the stairs, so Mimi and I can dart into our bathroom without running into them."

"Good idea."

"It's only for a few days, and it is lots of money," Phoebe said with an encouraging smile. "Now I must go upstairs and put the finishing touch on the hat Mrs. Roosevelt ordered for the in-auguration. Did I tell you what she said about it?"

"No."

"That she never wanted and still doesn't want to be a First Lady. Poor dear."

Chapter 2

At eight in the evening the phone rang and a voice that didn't sound like the man who had come to Grace and Favor earlier in the day asked Lily if the arrangement to hold a meeting at their home was satisfactory.

In spite of her own objections, she'd been clearly outvoted and was wondering if her imagination had really run away with her. She said yes, that the arrangement was all right. A few details of food preferences and available space were quickly worked out. The group would be coming there three days hence. Late Friday night. Perhaps staying only two days, not more than three. This person on the telephone, who hadn't given his name, sounded educated, pleasant, and sensible, which relieved Lily's fears a little.

The next morning, Robert hired the Harbinger boys to haul up a dining table and five straight-backed chairs from the extensive basements of Grace and Favor, clean them up, and move the enormous bed in the master bedroom to the far end of the room, under the windows.

Lily reported to Mrs. Prinney that one of the men coming didn't eat red meat but could eat fish or chicken. She also arranged for Mr. Prinney to put the cash, all but one fifty, in the safe at his office in town. They could certainly provide food and service with the remaining fifty-dollar bill.

This might work out well, Lily started thinking. The longer she considered, the more convinced she was that Phoebe had guessed correctly at the identity of the group. Politicians, especially frantic ones, had lots of money to spend. Some of them, especially the one in disguise, might be a public figure everyone had seen in the newsreels at the Voorburg movie house and could easily identify. The man she'd spoken to on the telephone seemed so efficient and well-bred, he couldn't possibly have anything to do with gangsters. Although Phoebe might be right and they could be Communists. Some of them were very well educated.

Lily was about to go upstairs to see how the furniture moving was going, when the front doorbell rang. A woman in her late fifties, with a neat gray bun and sensible shoes, introduced herself as the principal of the local grade school. "I'm Mrs. Betty Tarkington."

"I remember you, Mrs. Tarkington. We dispensed the potato salad at the Fate last summer," Lily said, using the villagers' pronunciation of *fête*.

"Does your brother happen to be available? I need to speak to him."

"Come in, please," Lily said. "He's not free right now. We're having guests in a day or two and he's moving a table and chairs around. Could I help you?"

Lily invited her into the library; its windows overlooked the Hudson River, and it was her favorite room in the sprawling mansion.

Mrs. Tarkington wandered toward the windows. "What a wonderful view you have here." She came back and sat down in a chair across from Lily's. "I've lost a teacher. Just temporarily. I think you also met her at the Fate. Miss Millicent Langston."

Lily smiled. It tickled her that even the school principal, who surely knew *Fate* wasn't the right pronunciation, used it as the other villagers did.

"The young woman who was telling us how much potato salad to put on each plate to make it last?" Lily asked.

Mrs. Tarkington nodded. "She usually makes herself memorable. But I received a telephone call from her saying the oddest thing. Apparently she has what she called a 'hot' appendix. It flares up every couple years and then it's all right again. She said the doctor in her hometown told her she should have it out when it wasn't infected. Less danger of complications. It seems he's about to move away and wanted her to come home and let him do the surgery before he left. Wouldn't trust the job to anyone else."

"So she left?"

"Just so. She said he told her it would take two or three weeks to fully recover."

"Where does my brother Robert come into this?"

"I was wondering if Mr. Brewster could be her substitute."

Lily wondered why Mrs. Tarkington had thought of Robert instead of herself, but didn't ask.

Mrs. Tarkington caught Lily's frown and guessed what she was thinking. "So many men are out of work these days."

"I see. I'll go fetch Robert for you, but he won't be able to do this for you for at least a week. Unless . . ."

"Unless what?"

"Could you divide the day up between Robert and me? For reasons I'm sorry I can't explain, Robert has to take breakfast, lunch, and dinner up to our guests."

Mrs. Tarkington thought for a moment. "I suppose that's a possibility."

"I could take the morning and lunchtime. Then Robert could take the afternoon. Dinner will be served long after school is dismissed. Excuse me for being realistic, but are you offering to pay us?"

"Of course. I was just about to say so."

"Let me find Robert and see if he's willing."

Robert and the Harbinger boys were just finishing up the furniture job. Lily told him, "We've been offered a teaching job at the grade school. The regular teacher has gone somewhere to have her appendix out."

"Dr. Polhemus isn't doing it, is he?" Robert asked with horror. The town doctor wasn't one of his favorite people. He was always gossiping about his patients' ailments to anyone who would listen.

"No, she went back to wherever she lives to have her own doctor do it. I thought I could take the morning through the lunchtime, and you could handle the afternoon classes."

"What are these classes you're assigning me to?"

"Come downstairs and we'll talk it over with Mrs. Tarkington."

When they entered the library, Mrs. Tarkington was looking over the bookshelves. "Are the books on all these locked shelves real books?" she asked.

"We don't think so," Robert said. "We believe they're just fake spines because they all look alike. But nobody has ever found the key to unlock the doors, and we can't afford a locksmith just to satisfy our curiosity."

"I think almost any of the boys in the fifth and sixth grade could do it for free," Mrs. Tarkington said with a laugh.

"Which grade would we be teaching?" Lily asked.

"Fifth and sixth. They're together. There aren't enough children to have a teacher for each grade."

Robert said, "You better get Lily to take care of the arithmetic. She's a whiz at numbers. I'm not. And she'd be a much better grammar teacher than I would."

Mrs. Tarkington nodded. "That would work out for the morning, Miss Brewster. And would you take on the short deportment lessons as well?"

"I'd be glad to. I didn't know grade schools did that."

"Most don't. But Miss Langston insisted and we've found it valuable. That would leave history, geography, and physical exercise for Mr. Brewster to handle."

Lily looked at Robert. "Right down your alley, Robert."

She addressed the principal. "My brother follows current and past events more studiously than I. And he's traveled more."

"What about this physical exercise thing?" Robert asked. "All I know is how to play polo."

Mrs. Tarkington smiled again. "We don't have horses, or even ponies, unfortunately. But we have a lot of hockey sticks and old croquet equipment. The boys, especially, need to run off a lot of their energy before they go home. Boys that age have altogether too much and put it to bad ends sometimes. And the girls tend to sit around and gossip and giggle if they don't have anything else to do."

"We'll be paid, Robert," Lily put in before he could ask.

*   *   *

When Mrs. Tarkington had gone back to school, Robert asked, "Who is this teacher and why did she leave?"

"It's Miss Millicent Langston. You remember her, don't you?"

"Oh, her! The woman who came to the Fate and wanted to see the whole mansion? What a nerve. Claiming you could learn a lot about people by the surroundings they chose to live in."

"She tried that on you, too?" Lily asked. "I told her I didn't have the time to show her around. Then she asked if she could just pop inside and go to the bathroom. I guess she didn't want to ask that of you."

"We should have pointed her to the woods instead of letting her in the house. Just on general principles."

Robert spent some of the afternoon at the town library. This was partly to visit with Miss Philomena Exley, the deliciously attractive young librarian. He needed a text on games as well. He vaguely remembered croquet but not the specific rules, and field hockey was something he knew nothing about. If he'd be teaching kids how to play, he'd better get it right. It sounded as if it were like polo without the horses. He wasn't sure of that.

"You're teaching for Miss Langston? Would you see that the children's books she's borrowed are returned? She seems to think they're hers to keep as long as she likes," Miss Exley said.

"Will do," Robert said. "When I master this croquet business, would you like to play a round or
two with me and my sister? Maybe on Saturday,
if it's warm enough?"

"That would be fun. But I don't know the rules
either. When I played it with my brothers, they
made up rules as they went along, so I always
lost. I'll count on you to tell us how to play."

Robert went back to Grace and Favor, thinking
this was the first "almost" date he'd had since late
October 1929. He didn't count the old ladies he'd
squired to Broadway plays and dinners during
the months between the Crash and when he and
Lily moved to Grace and Favor, rich dowagers
who had introduced him as a nephew instead of
what he really was—a paid gigolo.

Then he laughed at himself. What kind of date
was it when you invited your sister along? And
probably Mr. and Mrs. Prinney would play, as
well as whichever daughters and grandchildren
might be visiting on Saturday.

But it was a start. Maybe he'd invite Miss Exley
to the movie house when he received his first
payment for teaching.

He wondered what kind of movies a smart,
well-read woman like that would like.

Chapter 3

The next morning, Lily showed up at school extremely early. Mrs. Tarkington was the only other person in the building. "Let me show you the room you'll be using, Miss Brewster."

"How many are in this class?" Lily asked as the principal showed her the way.

"Fifth grade has two girls and four boys. Sixth grade has two girls and six boys."

"What accounts for the difference?"

"Just age."

"I meant, why are there only four girls and ten boys?"

"I'm sorry to say it, but most of the girls are helping their mothers. Many women who aren't educated themselves see no reason why their daughters need to be. Most people hereabouts believe only the boys need schooling to get jobs. It's a pity. At eleven and twelve, the girls are so much more receptive to learning. And if the economy isn't fixed soon, they're all going to have to try to acquire jobs to help support their families."

The schoolroom was old. The ancient desks and chairs were bolted to the floor, and generations had carved their names on the wooden desktops. Mrs. Tarkington had already made sure each child had a paper plaque at the front of their desks with his or her whole name printed on it.

"I thought it would make it a little easier for you to learn who is who," she said.

"How thoughtful of you. Thanks. Miss Langston must be very artistic. I like the pictures of the alphabet she's hung around the room with the pictures."

"For all her bossiness with adults, she's really an excellent teacher," Mrs. Tarkington said. "She simply doesn't know she shouldn't try to instruct people outside the classroom. She and a friend of hers share a house, and have a little business on the side selling needlework and embroidery patterns. They advertise in women's magazines. Miss Langston's grading book and lesson plans are in her desk."

The first children started filing in. Two girls, arm in arm. They sat down at their desks. Mrs. Tarkington said, "Mary Helene and Susie, don't be larking about that way. Sit in your own seats."

The girls giggled and exchanged places.

"I know you, Mary Helene," Lily said. "You're Mrs. Anderson's oldest girl, aren't you?"

"Yes, ma'am."

Roxanne Anderson's husband had died a few months ago, and Lily was glad to see that Mary

Helene was getting along so well and able to play little tricks with friends.

When all the children had arrived, Mrs. Tarkington introduced Miss Brewster and told the children that her brother, Mr. Brewster, would be teaching them in the afternoons.

"I'll leave it to you, now," she said, departing.

Lily said to the children, "Now I'd like to get to know you. Each stand up when I call on you, and tell me a little bit about yourself or your family. If you have pets. What your favorite subjects are. Whatever you'd like to say."

Two of the girls had cats that were from the same litter. Brothers, Mary Helene explained. She and a sixth-grade girl, Josie, were the cat owners. The other fifth-grade girl, Betsy, and her older sister, Susie, both mentioned that they had four younger brothers and a new baby on the way.

"Mommy's cried the whole time she was waiting," Betsy said. Susie nudged her to be quiet about that.

The boys had an assortment of pets to mention, mostly faithful old hunting dogs. The four boys in fifth grade—two of them named John and one Jim and a Ted—hardly mentioned their families or their favorite class. One sixth grader said his father had already taught him how to drive their old truck. He was allowed to do errands with it.

He's the top dog, Lily thought, watching the other boys, who obviously looked up to him for this. *I'll have to keep a good eye on him.*

"It's nice to know all of you," Lily told them with a smile. "Since I'm going to be teaching you English, arithmetic, and deportment, I'd like to know what you already know. I don't want to be repeating what you've already learned. Let's start with the times tables."

She called on them randomly, giving each a different set of one-digit numbers to multiply in their heads. Each answered quickly and correctly. "My goodness!" she exclaimed. "You're really a group of brainy kids."

Most of them smiled at her. Except for the boy who drove a truck. His name was Bob and he'd looked upset when she'd called him Bobby.

"Now I'll test you on addition." She gave each two double-digit numbers to add. A few of them, including a quiet sixth-grade boy named Hiram, had to think for a moment to carry over, but again, they all passed the test correctly.

"This is wonderful," Lily said. "We'll move on to grammar now." She wrote a sentence on the board for them to diagram on their tablets. A very simple one. When they all had it right, she gave them a slightly more complex one. All but two of the boys, Bob and Bill, succeeded, and neither of them were very far off. It obviously wasn't Bob's favorite challenge. Lily assumed he'd far rather be racketing around town in his father's truck.

She hardly needed to test them on deportment. She wasn't sure how she could anyway. They were all amazingly well mannered, with the exception of the slightly surly Bob.

They went back to their arithmetic books and started the lesson where Miss Langston had left a green ribbon marker in the teacher copy.

The morning seemed to fly by. Lily had never thought of being a teacher, but was enjoying herself with this well-behaved group of children. She gave them a short mid-morning break on whispered advice from one of the girls. After that she read to them aloud from a book on the desk that likewise had a green ribbon marker.

She hadn't read the book herself, so when something interesting happened in the plot and one of the younger boys, Ted, asked a question about it, she turned it over to his classmates to discuss.

After that she had them all get up and do a few stretching exercises because a few of them were looking tired and hungry. Then they went on to talk about how you should introduce people to each other.

She called Josie and Ted to the front of the room and said to Josie, "Mrs. Roosevelt, allow me to introduce you to Ted." Josie giggled and blushed and shook his hand.

"You always say the woman's name first, you see. Now, let's have Susie in place of Ted. Mrs. Roosevelt, I'd like to introduce you to Susie. The older woman's name first, especially when the older woman is far more famous."

She set them up in different combinations: older man to younger man, young woman to older man.

Lunch break followed this and they were all calling Josie "Mrs. Roosevelt" and opening doors for her to go first.

The school had a lunchroom but no kitchen, and all the children had brought food in their paper bags, which they carefully folded up to take home and use again. There was a refrigerator where milk was kept and a sink to wash out the cups they brought from home. Lily would have lunch at home, so she roamed around the room chatting with her students and noticed there was a difference in what came out of the bags.

Some had sandwiches with thick homemade bread and a meager slice of cheese. Others had more generous meals. A few children even had a peppermint or a lollipop for dessert. Lily observed that some of the larger, more substantial sandwiches were being shared with other children. Those who were a little better off had probably been told by their parents to do this.

Or maybe this was another of Miss Langston's deportment lessons.

They talked among themselves in the room where they ate. Lily soon realized they were talking about her from the badly concealed looks she was getting. They all seemed very cheerful about their substitute teacher, she guessed from their smiles.

Mrs. Tarkington came along and sat down beside her. "I must admit that I eavesdropped a bit on your class. You did an admirable job. Especially since you had so little time to prepare."

Lily posed a question. "I've never spent much time with children. Are these unusually polite and bright ones?"

"Not until Miss Langston started teaching them. And some of the boys aren't really tamed yet except when they're in class."

"That surprises me."

"Why?"

Lily tried to be tactful. "I've only met Miss Langston once and found her a bit of a—well—tartar."

She was afraid she'd offend, but Mrs. Tarkington smiled sadly. "She is, with adults. But she's really in her proper element with children. She's a natural-born teacher. She's firm and unrelenting, but sympathetic with the slower ones, mostly the boys. And she's remarkably kind and even sometimes humorous. I often hear them laughing in class. She's a very strange person, I have to admit. Socially inept around adults, and wonderful with children of this age. I'm not sure she could get along so well with very young children and would probably be a disaster with the older ones."

She glanced up and said, "Here's your brother. Ahead of time."

There was an undercurrent of excitement when Robert came into the lunchroom, especially with the girls, who giggled and blushed. "Your sister did a good job this morning," Mrs. Tarkington said to him. "I'm sure you will as well."

Robert ruffled through a wad of paperwork he had in his hand. "I've brushed up on croquet. And brought along some recent newspapers to have them read and discuss."

He looked as nervous as a cat on the Fourth of July.

But by the time he returned to Grace and Favor later that afternoon, he admitted, somewhat grudgingly, that he'd enjoyed his time. "The croquet equipment was too dirty to use, so I unearthed some badminton rackets and a net and a few bedraggled birds—or are they called pucks?—from the closet. Do you know what? The girls are better at badminton. The girls plan ahead. The boys simply bash away as hard as they can. Brains versus brawn, I imagine. Every one of them had fun, though."

"Including you?"

"Especially me," he said with a grin. "I'm among the bashers."

Chapter 4

Lily's and Robert's first day of teaching had been a Thursday, and they somehow managed to get through Friday without much more preparation. But Lily was hoping that the weekend would give her the opportunity to study what to teach the next week. And that went for Robert, too.

Grace and Favor was ready for the guests, who were due to arrive that evening. And all Robert had to do was deliver meals to the mysterious company. Mrs. Prinney, assuming they would have already eaten dinner, since they weren't arriving until after eight in the evening, only planned a light snack for their arrival. Nobody had mentioned liquor or beer, so she would serve only coffee and tea.

Lily wondered if the guests would stay through Tuesday, Election Day. If her own guess was correct about who they were and their secret agenda, they'd be sure to go back by then to wherever they came from, perhaps to spring their last-minute plan on the public. To persuade them to vote for Hoover when it was too late for Roosevelt's people to refute their arguments.

Friday afternoon before dinner, Robert asked, "Did anyone find the key to the meeting room? I've looked everywhere."

They'd had to remove the door from the hinges to get the table into the room, and the key had gone missing.

"Did you look under the throw rugs in the hall?" Phoebe Twinkle asked. "A key could have easily slipped under one."

"I took them all up," Robert said.

"It'll probably turn up somewhere," Lily said. "The head of the group will be staying in the room and presumably not leaving it. Unless he's a very heavy sleeper, he would hear if anyone came in. Or you could tell him to jam a chair under the knob."

"That's a cheap way to provide privacy," Robert said with a laugh.

"It is," Lily agreed. "But where are you going to find a locksmith before they arrive? It's too late."

Robert shrugged. "I guess I'll suggest the chair then. By the way, if it's warm enough Saturday afternoon, I'd like to invite you all to a croquet match on the back lawn. Miss Exley found a set of rules for me, and I invited her to come along."

"A date with Miss Exley?" Lily exclaimed.

"Not a date, really. Just a gathering to play a game or two and see if I have the hang of it well enough to teach the kids how to play correctly."

Lily and Phoebe exchanged conspiratorial smiles, but said nothing more.

Friday evening at eight was cool enough for light coats, but the guests arrived wearing heavy coats, hats, and mufflers that helped conceal their faces. The man who had arranged for the meeting was still wearing his dark glasses and awful wig. He made no attempt to introduce the members of the group.

"Just show us to the meeting room and the individual bedrooms and we'll be no trouble to you, except for meals," he mumbled through his muffler.

Robert led them up the stairs, showed them the adjoining third-floor bedrooms the men could choose, and came back downstairs.

"Nobody spoke, except the fellow with the bad wig. I left them to pick out their own rooms and explained about the missing key. The wigged gentleman didn't seem concerned, so I worried needlessly."

It was eerie having these strangers in the house, Lily thought. When you have guests, you're normally obligated to provide entertainment to them. Or at least converse with them. Not just allow them to hide in their rooms.

Robert loaded up the snack trays and trudged upstairs with them. He was told to leave them in the hallway by the man wearing the wig, who spoke through a mere crack of the door to the master suite. Robert had heard other voices talking very quietly before he knocked, but the others fell silent at his arrival.

"Strange folks," he muttered to himself as he went back down the stairs.

He found Lily and Phoebe in the library, gossiping mildly about Miss Langston.

"I wonder if it was female problems instead of this appendix story," Lily was saying to Phoebe.

Robert turned around and left the room. There was nothing on earth he'd rather *not* hear about.

"Could be," Phoebe allowed. "She might have been embarrassed to say so. I should be feeling sorry for her, but I can't."

"You've had trouble with her?"

"Over a hat, at least eventually," Phoebe said. "First she said she'd heard I lived upstairs above my shop. She wanted to see my rooms. Claimed that she could tell a lot about people's taste and character by seeing how they lived."

Phoebe went on, "I said it wasn't important what my tastes were. It was valuable to know hers, so why didn't we go look at where she lived? That made her mad to start with. She drew up a sketch of what she wanted, picked out a dark blue color for the hat and veil. Then brought it back because she thought the veil was too dark. She wanted me to return her money. I refused and she was really rude. And then she took an extra potshot at me for not cleaning the windows of the shop as often as I should. My shop was a blight on the landscape, she told me. And in these hard times it was especially important to keep up appearances. All it took was a bit of soap and water and ambition. Just as if I were one of the children who came to school with dirty hands."

"Apparently she gets away with that with the children. Mrs. Tarkington says they adore her, tough as she is. By the way, Roxanne Anderson's oldest girl is in my class. I'm glad she's determined that her girls be well educated. And not at all surprised. She's a tough woman as well. I wonder if for some reason Miss Langston doesn't come back if the school would consider hiring her instead. All she has to live on is her money from her gardening. And that's pretty much a summer job."

"If Miss Langston doesn't return pretty soon, you might suggest her," Phoebe said.

Saturday morning, after taking breakfast up to the guests, then fetching the trays and plates back, Robert went to work setting up the croquet court in the flat area behind the house, in spite of the fact that the weather had turned cloudy, windy, and cold.

"It's too cold for this," Lily said, in her coat and hat with her hands up her opposite sleeves.

"It'll warm up by this afternoon if the sun stays out," Robert said. "Don't you dare think of backing out. Even Mr. and Mrs. Prinney have agreed to play."

But it didn't warm up much. Miss Exley arrived, looking grand in an azure hand-knitted, belted, nubby wool coat with a matching hat. She looked very glamorous except for wearing golf shoes.

Robert refused to wear more than a light jacket over a sport coat and wool trousers. Lily was bundled up in her tatty sable coat and a pair of Mrs. Prinney's ghastly homemade, violently colored mittens and matching hat. Mrs. Prinney wore her old muskrat jacket, gloves, hat, and boots.

Robert explained the rules in great detail, which everyone ignored. Phoebe, who'd taken the afternoon off, was huddled on a lawn chair wrapped up in two afghans and was talking to Lily about Mrs. Governor Roosevelt having been in that morning to pick up her inauguration hat. "Poor dear lady, it's an awful hat, and yet she was really happy with it."

"Lily, are you listening to me?" Robert called to his sister.

"Not really. All that matters is that *you* know the rules," she said, abandoning Phoebe and picking up a mallet.

"Not that one," Robert said. "Your mallet and balls are the green ones."

"Why?"

"They just *are*! Take my word for it."

Within half an hour Robert was nearly berserk.

"You're all cheating," he said. "And that dog isn't helping."

Lily's dog, Agatha, was trying to get the balls in her mouth, slobbering all over them and moving them around. She was also nipping at mallets and trying to squeeze through the hoops and knocking them down.

"We're cheating to make this game end," Lily said. "We're all freezing to death."

Mrs. Prinney had given up early, citing the excuse that she had to start dinner for their guests. Phoebe had simply disappeared with no explanation at all. Miss Exley said she had to go home to take a steaming hot bath before she came down with a cold.

Robert, whose hands were so freezing they were numb, nevertheless gave up with bad grace. "All right. I guess Agatha and I are the only ones having fun," he said, starting to gather up the croquet paraphernalia to return to the school on Monday. He was as grumpy as a child who hadn't gotten enough sleep. This was rare behavior. Except when he was talking politics, he was normally cheerful.

Lily and Mr. Prinney fled, and Lily called Agatha inside, petting her and saying, "Good dog."

Robert went up to the room where the men were having their meeting and asked if they needed a fire made. "The furnace doesn't work all that well up here."

He was told, again through a mere crack in the door, but this time by a young man who spoke well and was no longer in disguise, that he could just leave some firewood by the door and he'd take care of it.

"Would you like to help me carry it up?" Robert asked, a bit put out. He hadn't anticipated this being part of the job.

"I'm sorry, but I can't," the young man said, sounding genuinely regretful, as if he'd rather fetch wood than sit in the meeting.

Robert hauled two loads from the backyard and then went back for a third load for himself, lit the fireplace in his own room, and took a long hot bath.

At dinner, Phoebe said, "I heard those men doing a sort of chant when I went up the stairs."

Robert smiled. "The stairs don't go anywhere near their room."

Phoebe blushed. "No. I was just snooping, I admit."

"What sort of chant?" Lily asked, taking a second helping of the delicious pork roast Mrs. Prinney had made.

"They were doing it so quietly, I couldn't tell."

"I'll bet they're rehearsing some sort of nasty political chant they've come up with in sheer desperation," Robert speculated. "I actually saw one of them without the disguise when I took their dinner up. A respectable looking chap."

"Did they mention when they're leaving?" Mrs. Prinney asked, her mind on food. She had enough to feed them through Sunday, Monday, and Tuesday breakfast, but not Tuesday lunch.

"Not a word," Robert replied, little knowing how very much longer they'd end up involving the residents of Grace and Favor—against everyone's choice.

Chapter 5

Early Sunday morning, Lily was going down the second-floor hall on her way to help Mrs. Prinney prepare breakfast for the guests. As she approached the stairway, a young man burst out of the master suite. He was a good-looking blond fellow about Lily's age, in a dark blue and red dressing gown with sleep creases on the left side of his face.

"Miss Brewster," he said, running to meet her, "call the police, please. Our employer is dead. Murdered."

He ran back to the suite without another word.

Lily immediately went downstairs and did as he asked. Chief of Police Howard Walker answered sleepily.

"It's Lily Brewster. A guest here says another guest has been murdered," she told him.

"Who is the victim?" Walker asked. His voice was muffled because he was trying to get dressed even as he was speaking to her.

"I have no idea what their names are," Lily admitted.

"You don't know the names of the people who are in your house?"

"I'll explain that later. Shall I call Dr. Polhemus?"

"I'll call him, Lily, and then I'll come right over. Stay calm."

Lily went to the kitchen to speak to Mrs. Prinney and said only that one of the guests had died. "Apparently we won't be serving breakfast for a while. Chief Walker and Dr. Polhemus are on the way. I'll wait at the door for Howard."

As she waited, the blond young man came rushing down the stairs. He was now dressed but his tie was askew. He'd smoothed down his hair and apparently had tried to shave, but had nicked up half of his face and given up. He was now wearing small gold spectacles. "Are the police on the way, Miss Brewster?"

"Yes. Who are you?" It was time she learned some of their names.

"Edward Price, Miss Brewster. I'm the one who spoke to you on the phone."

"Yes, I recognize your voice, but you never told me who you were."

"Why's it taking the police so long to get here?" He had taken his glasses off and was ineffectively trying to clean them with his handkerchief. He looked as if he were a highly upset professor. In fact, he looked vaguely familiar, like someone she'd met. Where would she have met him?

"He has to drive up here from town. I think I

hear his car now." Coatless, they both stepped out the front door.

Howard Walker had done a better job of throwing on his clothes than Edward Price had, but he hadn't bothered to shave and looked quite fierce. He was a relative newcomer to Voorburg. He had one Delaware Indian in his heritage, who had married into a Dutch family in a nearby town. Walker's appearance was a genetic throwback to the Indian. A very handsome man, nearing thirty, with thick black hair, he was a favorite of the ladies in town, not only because of his looks, but also due to his good manners.

He glanced at the fair-haired young man and pulled Lily aside to whisper, "Lily, I couldn't find Ralph. Could you come with me to take notes? I don't want to be scribbling down what people say. I want to be looking at them like a hawk."

Lily stared at him.

"You won't have to look at the body," Walker reassured her. He then approached the young man. "Where's the body? And who is it?"

Edward Price replied, "It's Charles Pottinger. You'll have heard of him as Brother Mark Luke Goodheart."

"The radio preacher?" Lily asked.

Price nodded, and as the three of them started upstairs, he introduced himself by name to Chief Walker and said he was Brother Goodheart's secretary.

Lily stood outside the door to the master suite

while Walker took a look at the body. The other guests began appearing in the hall. "What's going on?" asked an elderly, highly scarred man with a very lumpy visage and a gravelly voice.

"I don't think I'm allowed to say, but I believe you ought to go back to your own rooms for a while. Someone's been injured."

As if summoned by this remark, Dr. Polhemus, the town doctor, joined the group, saying cheerfully, "Lily, you left the front door open. Walker's told me he's got another stiff." And without another word, he went into the suite, shutting the door firmly behind him.

"A stiff!" the old man exclaimed. "Who's dead?"

"The chief of police will tell you later," Lily said to the group. "Please go back to your rooms."

As soon as they wandered up to the third floor, heads together, whispering, Lily ran down the hall and roused Robert.

"Get dressed as fast as you can and guard the stairs. Our main guest, who turns out to be that nasty radio guy Brother Goodheart, is dead, and I've made his cronies go back to their rooms. I have to take notes for Howard Walker, and someone needs to see that none of the others try to make a break for it."

Robert was already putting his trousers on over his pajama pants. "Brother Goodheart! I can't believe we let that man in the house. Pretty Boy Floyd would have been a more welcome choice."

As Lily headed back down the hall, one of the other guests was, in fact, trying to depart, suitcase in hand.

"Get back to your room right now!" Lily snapped.

His mouth opened, but no words came. He merely scowled and did as she said.

As a disheveled Robert joined her, she told him that one of their guests, a heavy man with dark reddish hair, had already attempted to bolt. A moment later Walker opened the door and asked Lily to come inside.

"Robert's standing guard," she explained. "I sent the rest of them upstairs and one has already tried to get away."

She entered the room, half expecting, against what Walker promised, to see a corpse. But there wasn't one.

She sat down next to Walker at the head of the big table and reached for one of the notepads the men had apparently brought with them. Walker stopped her hand before she picked it up, and tore out the blank pages at the back of the pad and handed her one of the pens on the table.

"Okay, Mr. Price. Tell me about this," Walker said.

Edward Price was sitting hunched over on a chair in the corner. Lily hadn't even noticed him. He stood up, took a deep breath, and joined them at the table, sitting opposite Lily.

"Where do you want me to start?" he asked.

"For now, when you found the body," Walker replied.

"I was sleeping in the servant's room beyond the hall and the bathroom. I opened the bathroom door and saw him in the tub. I was nearly sick in the sink. I went for help, ran into Miss Brewster, and asked her to call you."

"You knew he was dead? You didn't try to help him?"

Edward Price snorted. "With a knife in his back, bent forward with his head in the water, which was all red? Of course I knew he was dead and must have been for quite a while. The room wasn't even steamy and it was quite cold in there."

"I noticed," Walker said with what might have been sarcasm. "The room is cold and so is he. He's been in there most of the night, I'd guess. Did you hear anything from the next room overnight?"

Before Price could reply, Dr. Polhemus came through from the hallway, drying his hands on a towel. "I suspect the damage to the spinal cord that high paralyzed him, but the immediate cause of death is probably drowning. I'll send someone to fetch him and do an autopsy in any case."

Lily felt faint and knew she'd probably gone as pale as Edward Price.

As Dr. Polhemus left, Walker asked briskly, "Miss Brewster, where were we?"

She pulled herself together and read his last

question to Price. " 'Did you hear anything from the next room?' "

Price, still working at regaining his composure, said, "Not a thing, but then I wouldn't. I'm a heavy sleeper and I like to be in a cold room with a window open and covered with as many blankets as I can find."

"But you shaved," Walker observed.

Price shrugged, embarrassed. "Somehow it seemed to me, bizarrely, I admit, the respectful thing to do, and I thought I could do it without looking at him. But I couldn't finish." He put his hand up to his cheek and noticed that he was bleeding a bit and mopped the side of his face with his handkerchief.

Walker asked him to turn his head and examined his cheek closely. "Well, at least it really is your own blood. When did you go to bed?"

"Around ten, maybe quarter after," Price said, still dabbing at his face.

"And you heard nothing?" Walker asked again.

"I heard him running the bath and that's all. It's a habit of his to take a really hot bath before he goes to bed. At the Institute, the man in the room below his goes nearly mad because when the tub drains it makes a banging, gurgling noise in his room. You can ask the others about this. Everyone knows Brother Goodheart's habits."

He looked at Lily taking down what he said. "Really," Price added somewhat desperately.

"What's your connection with this man? Didn't you say you were his secretary?"

"A dogsbody really. I'm a former English professor but my college went bankrupt. All I do is correct the grammar in the speeches he writes and type them up."

"Did you like the man?"

Price took a deep breath and said quietly, "I despised his vulgarity. I hated every word he said. Even his appearance, voice, and the smell of the cologne he used revolted me. But well-paid jobs aren't thick on the ground these days. I didn't kill him. I'll tell you anything you need to know, but I swear I didn't do it."

The questioning was delayed by a noisy scuffle in the hall. When Walker opened the door, it was to the sight of Robert, striped pajamas like little petticoats escaping from the bottom of his trousers. He was holding the ginger-haired man by one arm and pinning the other one behind the man's back.

"Another one decided to hippity-hop home," Robert said.

Chapter 6

While the interview with Edward Price was going on, Mr. Prinney was in his office at Grace and Favor with Mary Towerton. She'd used her mule and cart to drive over from her small farm outside Voorburg with her children. Mrs. Prinney had them in the kitchen and was giving Mary's little boy bread and jam and hand-feeding the baby girl some pablum she kept for her grandchildren.

"I'm so sorry to bother you at home, Mr. Prinney, and on a Sunday, but I've received an alarming telegram and I don't know how to respond," Mary said, handing him the piece of paper.

He read it with a frown. "I'm so sorry," he said.

The telegram was to alert her that her husband had died of pneumonia. It said that he had been working in the tunnels that were going to divert the Colorado River so work could commence on the building of Hoover Dam. It went on to say he could be buried there, or his body could be shipped to her home for burial.

"Which are you going to do? Bury him here or there?" Mr. Prinney asked.

"That's not really the problem. I simply can't afford to bury him here. I haven't even found the money to move my grandfather from his grave in Maryland. You see, they have his name wrong. He's Richard Towerton and this telegram calls him Rick Taughton."

"Oh, I didn't even notice that. It's addressed to you by the name Taughton as well."

"You see, I don't know if this is my own husband or not. They might have made a mistake. This may not even be my husband."

"When did you last hear from him?" Mr. Prinney asked.

"A year and a half ago when he was leaving on the train."

"He hasn't written you?"

"He can't read or write," Mary admitted.

Mr. Prinney steepled his fingers and thought for a while. "Is it possible that when he gave his name, whoever wrote it down misunderstood what he said and he wasn't equipped to correct it?"

"I've wondered if that was the case. I need your advice. It isn't the burial that's important right now. I suppose it's already been taken care of. It's whether I'm a widow or a wife. What can I do?"

"Leave it to me," Mr. Prinney said. "As your attorney, I'll send a telegram back pointing out the error in spelling and saying I'm sending a picture of him to see if it matches the man who died. You do have a photograph of him, don't you?"

"Only our wedding picture. Would I get it back?"

"I regret to say I couldn't promise that. Could you describe him?"

Mary thought for a moment. "He's about six inches taller than I. Dark brown hair, brown eyes. He has a crooked nose and a bad scar on his mouth from an accident on his old tractor."

Mr. Prinney wrote this down, but didn't say what he was thinking. If Mrs. Towerton's husband had been killed in an explosion, instead of dying of pneumonia as the telegram said, his face might not even be recognizable. And if he was so uneducated and had a large enough scar on his lip, he might not have been able to speak clearly enough to be understood well.

"I'll send the telegram tomorrow with the description. Bring me the wedding photograph and let me see if someone in Poughkeepsie can make a good copy."

"I hate to put you to that trouble. I'll gladly pay for your time and effort."

"Tell me a bit about yourself. How do you support your family? Are all or part of his wages sent to you?"

"No. My grandfather left me money in a tin hidden beside the fireplace. Not a lot, but enough to live on comfortably. When Richard's father died, he was the only child and sold the farm. We bought my grandfather's house with the money. Of course, we expected Grandfather to move out and get his own place closer to town."

Mr. Prinney was familiar with old Joe Wyman and figured she meant closer to the town speakeasy in the back room of Mabel's Cafe, where he'd spent most of his time getting mean drunk.

"But he stayed on with us," Mary said, "saying he wouldn't spend the money we gave him for the house and it would come back to us. Richard knew that and was going to save all the money he made and bring it back when the dam was finished. I also hand-sew baby clothes. I give some of them away to the less fortunate families and sell the rest to a shop in Philadelphia."

"They must be exceptional," Mr. Prinney said politely.

"They are. It's my only talent. Phoebe Twinkle supplies me with lacy trim and ribbons for the ones I sell."

She paused and then said, as if ashamed to ask, "If it is my husband, will I get the money he saved? The telegram doesn't say. Grandpa's money won't last me forever."

"I'll ask about this when I send the photograph. I know very little about the building of this dam, but I've heard the working conditions in the tunnels are very dangerous. The dust creates explosions. Since he might have died in an accident at work, you might be entitled to monetary com-

pensation as well. I'm loath to ask you this, but
are you absolutely certain that's where he went?"

"Of course," she said, but there was a hint of
doubt in her voice. "I know a lot of women's
husbands have abandoned them, but I don't
think Richard just ran away. Of course, neither
of us knew about little Emily being on her way
when he left. He was very upset about the tractor being repossessed because Grandpa
wouldn't pay to fix it. And the fact that we had
to live in my grandfather's house with him.
Grandpa was a difficult person to live with and
was always criticizing Richard. It didn't bother
Richard as much as it did me, but Grandpa was
so nasty to him in front of my little boy Joey that
it nearly drove me mad."

"Emily is your baby?"

"Yes. It's Richard's late mother's name," she
said, her voice breaking and a tear running down
her face.

Mr. Prinney sat awhile when Mrs. Towerton had
left. He was thinking, somewhat guiltily, that she
might be better off if this Taughton person who
died really was her husband. She was a pretty
young woman, with long blond hair in a braid
around her head. She had two pretty children
and was obviously well educated, judging by her
grammar. She was talented and knew how to
take care of money. If she were widowed, she
could make a much better second marriage to a

man of her own quality, instead of being saddled with an illiterate, seemingly unattractive husband who might have simply walked out on his responsibilities.

He certainly wouldn't charge her for helping. This was a moral dilemma just as much as a legal one. And there was nothing he could do about it today. The nearest telegraph office was in Poughkeepsie, which was also the only place he might be able to get the photograph copied.

Meanwhile, there was a dead man upstairs to be dealt with.

"What was the purpose of this secret meeting?" Chief Howard Walker was asking Edward Price at the same time.

"It's in the nature of a palace coup."

"What does that mean?" Walker asked.

"It's complicated. Brother Goodheart is under attack, and rightly so, in my opinion. You know those film things he does where he hauls a bedraggled family up to the podium and they thank him effusively for his 'divine help' with their medical or financial troubles? The man is toothless, the woman is skinny, and the kids are cute as buttons?"

"I've seen that on the newsreels at the movie house," Walker acknowledged.

"Well, these people are carefully picked, carefully rehearsed. And he leads people to think they're just a few of the unfortunate multitudes he's helped out. But it's not true. He's making a fortune on these preaching campaigns."

"So it's a money matter," Walker said, nodding. "Not surprisingly."

Price ran his hand through his hair, messing it up. Lily looked at him and thought once again that he was strangely familiar. Had she seen him before, or did he simply remind her of someone else? She'd been vaguely aware of this since she first saw him.

Price went on, "The man who's caused this meeting is the only important one to the Institute who isn't here."

"Hold up. What institute? That's the second time you've used that term," Walker said.

Price looked disgusted. "That's what Goodheart calls his outfit. The Institute of Divine Intervention."

"How pretentious," Lily muttered.

Walker looked at her. "Please just take notes, Miss Brewster."

It was a fair shot, Lily had to admit. She was here to do a job. Not to make comments. She was feeling a bit smug anyway about this note taking. A month earlier she'd checked out a book from the library to learn shorthand and she was certainly no expert, but she was able to put what little she'd already learned to good use.

"So who is behind this meeting?" Walker continued.

"Big Jimmy Rennie. He's the treasurer of the Institute. He knows, as almost everyone with any brains does, that Brother Goodheart is using a lot of the money he collects for his own uses. Fancy cars, expensive hotels, and inappropriate women he hires for his own pleasure." Price actually blushed.

He went on. "I suspect, but don't have proof, that Big Jimmy himself has a hand in the till as well. In the last year he's bought a new car, much bigger and more expensive than he had before, and he's dressing a lot better. But that's beside the main point. Rennie's been subtly suggesting to Brother Goodheart that his conscience, such as it is, might force him to reveal Goodheart's spending habits. This would leave Rennie in charge of the whole bundle."

Lily was again tempted to comment, but Walker said what she was thinking.

"Wouldn't that bring the whole outfit down in a heap? Put everybody out of a job?" Walker asked.

"Probably so. But both of them are already rich and can go on to another scam, I presume. But they're both greedy bastards—pardon my language, Miss Brewster—and the rest of us involved know we have to support Goodheart to keep our salaries. Goodheart is—or was—a very stupid man. When we all disappeared at the same time, Big Jimmy certainly figured out what was happening."

"And may have known where you were going for the meeting?"

"Possibly. He has his own loyal toadies at the Institute."

They were again interrupted, this time by the arrival of two men in grubby white uniforms coming to take away the body.

"Stand by while I get everyone out of the way," Walker told them. "Lily, will you ask Robert to herd all the other members of this group into the dining room for breakfast and keep an eye on them. Is Mrs. Prinney ready to serve it? I don't want gawkers. And see if you can find Harry Harbinger, or better yet, Ralph Summer, and ask him to come help me out here."

"I'll do so," Lily said. She was glad to escape. She didn't want to watch the removal of the body.

Chapter 7

Lily couldn't find Ralph Summer but was lucky and located Harry Harbinger very easily. He showed up almost immediately to act as guard on the guests who were confined to the dining room. Harry locked the doors to the outside. It was virtually the only big room at Grace and Favor that had locks on the windows. Harry stood in the doorway to the front hall, watching the guests.

He didn't ask questions, just did what he was told. He was a big, strong young man. That was all that was needed to keep them in place.

Walker called the Newburg police station, which was the one closest to the Institute of Divine Intervention. He asked their chief of police, Leland Colling, whom he'd met several times and believed to be responsible, to pick up Big Jimmy Rennie and hold him until he could find someone to fetch him to Voorburg.

"On what charge?" Colling asked.

"For questioning in the murder of Brother Goodheart," Walker said.

"Wow!" Colling said. "This saves me the trouble of bumping him off myself," he added with a laugh. "You have no idea what a nuisance it is to have those people on our doorstep."

Walker smiled and added, "Get a warrant to search and seize every single financial document and box them securely. Keep what you box at the local jail until I find someone in the state treasurer's office in Albany to pick them up."

"I have a fingerprinting expert here for a couple days to teach my staff about it," Chief Colling said. "Want to borrow him?"

"It couldn't hurt. Thanks, Leland."

Howard Walker was fortunate to not only have a job, but have a deputy as well. Many of the smaller towns up and down the Hudson River Valley didn't even have a police force. So it was common for small towns to call on the larger ones like Beacon, Poughkeepsie, and Newburg for extra help when they needed it.

Keeping these four people confined and searching the Institute's records was going to require more people than he had, even with Harry Harbinger as a part-time deputy. And more than his budget would allow.

Walker went back to the master suite and, with Lily still taking notes, continued to question Edward Price.

Walker was glad the younger man was willing to cooperate, but he felt contempt for him. Walker didn't believe that these hard times justified bending your own moral rules and conscience just to have a job. To be fair, Walker had a reasonably good job himself. A job he genuinely liked.

Robert brought up a tray of food and sat in on the interview. He was the only one eating enthusiastically. Walker and Price ignored the breakfast. Lily only picked at the eggs awkwardly with her left hand while she took notes with the right.

"Tell me about the others. Start with the big redheaded guy who tried to leave," Walker said.

"He's Jackson Kinsey," Edward Price said. "Goodheart's personal attorney. Disbarred in Vermont, or somewhere up there, but qualified in New York State. He's bright but entirely without ethics."

Walker cast a dour look at Price, thinking this young man had no room to complain. "Why do you think he tried to bolt?"

"I suppose to go to the Institute and snatch all the paperwork, especially the financial papers."

"He won't see any of them until this goes to trial," Walker remarked.

Robert butted in to say, "I guess Brother Goodheart won't be doing his Sunday morning rant on the radio."

"Yes, he will," Price said. "He records all his talks on one of those tubular recording gadgets and somebody up there will probably have the wit to replay one of them near the microphone."

Walker glared at Robert, who went back to eating his breakfast.

"Who is the one with the awful face?" Walker asked.

"I don't know his real name. We all call him Nobby Hazard. He and Goodheart go way back. His looks are because he grew up in an orphanage and had smallpox as a child, he says."

"What is his job?"

"He arranges all the transportation, hires the people who set up the stages when Goodheart's doing his tours. Books the hotels where they stay. He's the only one who's absolutely loyal to Goodheart. He's abrasive and tough. Someone told me he used to be a fire-and-brimstone preacher himself, but his looks were against him, so he attached himself to Goodheart years ago because he believed in him."

"And did he know that Goodheart was keeping most of the money he raised?" Walker asked.

"I don't know. I doubt it. He's only concerned with bringing as many people into the fold as he can. He does all the promotional flyers as well. I go through them and correct the spelling and grammar even though the content makes me feel sick at heart."

"But if he did know, how would he react?"

Price's eyebrows went up. "He'd kill the bastard for betraying him."

"That's all I need from you now, Mr. Price. You can stay here and eat your breakfast. Don't even think of leaving the house." Walker took Lily with him.

"Miss Brewster," he said as they went downstairs, "I'm going to have to keep these people here for a while. We have only one jail cell, as you know, and there is a drunk driver in it right now. I know it's an inconvenience. But maybe I can talk the city into at least paying for their food until I figure out where else to put them. I'd also suggest strongly that you get good locks on all the doors to Grace and Favor. Any one of those men could have killed Goodheart, or it could have been someone like this Rennie person walking in one of the doors."

"You'll have to say that to Mr. Prinney yourself," Lily responded. "We've been nagging him for ages about locks. But he says there are too many doors and windows on the ground floor to afford to get all new locks. He nearly had a stroke when we redid the third floor and put locks on those doors."

"But there wasn't one on the door to the master suite?"

"There was, but Robert had to take the door off to get the big table in there and the key went missing. I think they told Goodheart he'd have to put a chair under the door to secure it."

"I wonder if he did."

"That would leave only Edward Price as a suspect."

"I know. But the way he's spilling his guts, such as they are, I don't think he did it. He'd have been too afraid of losing his job. I'll have a word with Mr. Prinney. Maybe this murder will change his mind about locks and keys."

* * *

But Mr. Prinney was busy with Mary Towerton and told Walker he'd have to wait a while. Mary had come back with the wedding picture showing her husband and herself. She was still reluctant to part with it, but Mr. Prinney said, "I remembered after you left that I know a man in Poughkeepsie who has a lot of photographic equipment. I handled his rental contract when he started the business. I've already phoned him at home and asked him to be waiting for me to bring the photograph tomorrow morning. I won't come home until I have the copy and yours."

"It's so good of you to do this for me. I know I'm taking you away from other work. At least let me give you some money," Mary said, pulling some well-worn bills out of her pocket.

"No, I'll just take care of it. Keep your money for your children. I can't promise you a result. If I am successful, you can repay me with a fancy baby dress for my next grandchild."

"I'll start a new one tomorrow."

Mr. Prinney smiled. "The next one isn't due until February."

She put her money back in her pocket reluctantly and said, "I left the children in the front hall. I must get back to them. Thank you again, Mr. Prinney."

He hadn't yet looked at the picture she'd brought when he heard the wagon leave. Now he stared at it. Her husband, in his best clothes, even without the broken nose and scar on his lip that he acquired after the marriage, was an ordinary looking chap. A little sullen, perhaps. Or maybe just scared of what he'd done.

Mrs. Towerton was standing behind him, one hand on his shoulder, the other holding her bouquet, and she was smiling. She looked a little bit like his eldest daughter had at the same age, before she married and put on weight.

There was a knock on the door and, putting away the picture with the telegram, he called, "Come in. Oh, Chief Walker, I was just getting ready to look for you."

Walker took the chair across the desk from the attorney. "First, I think the earlier experience of finding a body in the kitchen of this house, combined with this murder, should convince you to get locks on all the doors and windows on the ground floor."

Mr. Prinney nodded. "So you think someone might have gotten into the house?"

"It's possible."

"But improbable, I'd guess."

"I don't know much yet about the people who were here," Walker said. "Except that they represent an organization in disarray. Until I interview them, and everyone they left behind, I won't know who had the motive and no alibi. But common sense demands locks anyway."

"Where are you taking these invaders of our hospitality?"

Walker said, "Nowhere yet. I'm going to have to leave them here under guard until I can find a nearby jail that can take them. I'm even considering Matteawan."

"The place for the criminally insane?"

"As far as I'm concerned, they *are* criminally insane," Walker said. "I can probably pop them in there for evaluations for a couple days. Meanwhile, Harry Harbinger, Ralph Summer—if I can find him—and I will take turns at the head of the stairs on the third floor. If I need to, I'll borrow some other help from somewhere. I already have Newburg's department seizing the records and loaning us a fingerprint expert. We're going to have to search the entire mansion. Do I need a warrant?"

Walker knew, as did everyone in town, that Lily and Robert didn't really own Grace and Favor. Important decisions fell to Mr. Prinney as the executor of the Brewsters' great-uncle's estate.

Mr. Prinney was appalled. "A warrant? Of course not. Those of us who live here need to know who did this as much as you do. But how long will it be before you take them all away? One of them is probably a murderer."

"Not more than two days, I hope. I don't relish the thought of sitting in the hallway on my shift for longer than that. I wish it weren't a Sunday. I'll need to get hold of someone in Albany to examine their finances. This appears to be all about vast sums of money."

Chapter 8

The morning wore on endlessly. Walker received a phone call from Chief Colling. "This blabber-mouth Jimmy Rennie is driving us mad. I'm going to send him to you with two big guys. You can keep one of them if you need an extra deputy. I'll pay for his time. It's worth every cent to quiet down Rennie's yap."

Walker had interviewed Jackson Kinsey, Good-heart's attorney, and got nowhere. He was the one Robert had caught trying to leave Grace and Favor. "Why were you trying to leave?" was Walker's first question.

"I have nothing to say about that," Kinsey said. His face was almost as red as his hair, and his head seemed physically bigger than the normal person's. The man was determined not to reveal anything.

"You're Goodheart's attorney, aren't you? Or maybe I should be calling him by his real name, Charles Pottinger, I believe."

"Who my clients are is my business, not yours."

"We've taken Big Jimmy Rennie into custody and seized all the paperwork at the Institute," Walker told Kinsey.

"That's not legal," Kinsey said, pounding his big hairy fist on the large table in the master suite. "You'll regret this, you tin-pot despot."

"I believe it is legal. We'll all find out eventually, won't we?" Walker said with a smile. "Tin-pot despot" was a phrase that had never yet been applied to him, and it amused him to hear it from Kinsey, of all people.

Walker gave up on him for the time being and said, "You're free to go back to your room. A deputy will tell you when luncheon is served."

Kinsey huffed his way out of the suite and to his own room under Robert's close watch.

When Robert returned, Walker said, "Would you bring me this Nobby Hazard, please."

Nobby soon appeared, spiffed up to his poor best. The old man was in a black suit that had seen better decades and wore a stiff celluloid collar that had yellowed with age. His skimpy gray hair was greased down and had a knife-edge part in the middle. Whatever the grease was, it stank. He had a thin, wrinkled face with many old smallpox knobs and depressions, and his mean little blue eyes were set very close together.

"What do you want with me?" he said, perching upright on the chair at the corner of the table. His feet were lined up primly in old-fashioned black patent shoes with cracks across the toes.

"I need to know what your job is at the Institute," Walker said as pleasantly as he could manage.

"Why?"

"Because your boss has been murdered and I need to know who did it and why. My investigation involves asking everybody lots of nosy questions, Mr. Hazard."

"Reverend Hazard," Nobby said.

"Everyone else calls you Nobby, don't they?"

The old man frowned but didn't reply.

"Your job?" Walker persisted.

"I make—made—all the travel plans when Brother Goodheart did his preaching missions."

Walker already knew this from Edward Price, but was surprised that Pottinger/Goodheart had sent such an unpleasant looking person to set up his speaking engagements. Why would he have chosen Nobby?

"Did you handle the money collected at these events?" Walker asked.

"No. Brother Goodheart assigned trusted employees of the Institute in the audience to collect the money in baskets made at the Institute. The baskets were then raffled off after the money was turned over to him. It all went into a sturdy Gladstone bag he kept under the podium."

"Then where did it go?"

"Back to the Institute with him in his private car."

"With you in the car?"

"No, Brother Goodheart always had his own driver. He'd leave me enough cash to pay for the hotel and food and incidentals and I'd follow later on a train or boat to the next place he was speaking or back to the Institute."

"And who was the driver?"

"It wasn't never the same person. He always hired somebody from the town we were in and paid the driver's way back home."

Walker thought that was damned clever of the crooked preacher. Nobody knew what Goodheart was doing in the back of the car. If the current driver had suspicions of the furtive sound of paper money whispering its way out of the bag, he'd have nobody he knew to consult about those thoughts.

"Would it surprise you to know that Brother Goodheart was skimming money out of the proceeds before turning the bag over to Big Jimmy Rennie?"

This enraged the old man. His face turned into a mask of hatred. He raised a fist like a prophet. "Never! *Never!* You liar! You just ain't Christian enough to understand what a great man Brother Goodheart was. You're jealous of him. You wish you was as beloved as he was. He helped thousands of poor people by sharing others' wealth with them to help them live better lives. God above will curse you to hell and damnation for even thinking such a thing."

Robert poked his head in the door to see what the ruckus was about. Walker waved him away.

"Isn't that exactly what the meeting was about?"

"No, it was about Big Jimmy's accusations of the same thing. Big Jimmy will rot in hell with you."

"You never considered that Big Jimmy might have been right?"

"Not in a million years. Big Jimmy was the godless crook who was pilfering the money and threatening to blacken Brother Goodheart's name. I've prayed for his holy punishment like I'll pray for yours."

He proceeded to do so, standing upright, hands thrown up to his vengeful God and pontificating at the top of his lungs. "Dear Lord above, take away these sinners with their evil, despicable, dried-up hearts!"

Walker rose and strolled around the table while this performance went on and on, getting uglier by the minute. Finally he said, "Save the raving, Nobby, old boy."

Nobby Hazard ignored him and pitched his voice up a notch. As he did, he started speaking in tongues.

Walker opened the door and steered the old man out into the hall. "Robert, would you put him back in his own room?"

The voice continued to rant, echoing through the halls of Grace and Favor as Nobby was led away.

Mr. Prinney came up from the main floor, alarmed. "What on earth . . . ?"

"Just a dotty old man who can't face what's probably the truth."

"You must get these people out of this house. This is an abomination to decent people," Mr. Prinney said, sounding a little like Nobby himself.

Walker sighed. "I'll try to get in touch with someone at Matteawan to take them away as soon as possible. May I use your phone? I doubt that anyone in authority is there today, but I'll see what I can do."

His prediction was correct. He reached the assistant director of the Asylum for the Criminally Insane in Beacon, who said he'd have to get the permission of the director.

"Give me his home telephone number, please," Walker said.

"I can't give that out," the assistant claimed.

"You're dealing with the police, sir. Give me the number."

The assistant caved in. "Oh, in that case . . ."

The director, when reached, was reluctantly agreeable. "We're awfully full up right now, Chief Walker. And we can only hold them for three days, maybe four, while they're examined for both insanity and criminal intent or actions. How many do you have?"

"Only two at the moment," Walker said, mentally excusing Edward Price as the most important witness to keep close at hand. "There will probably be a third by the end of the day. Have you the transportation to fetch them?"

"The loony truck? Yes, but I'll have to round up a driver and a guard. That will take me a good hour or two. Give me the address where they're to be picked up."

Walker smiled to himself. This seemed such a routine job to the man he was speaking to. Who would have thought? He gave the instructions for finding Grace and Favor.

"Good. That's quite close to us, fortunately."

Mr. Prinney had been eavesdropping and was relieved.

Lunch was way overdue, Walker realized because his stomach had started growling. As he went down the stairs to the main floor, Ralph Summer came to the front door.

"You been looking for me, Chief?"

"Where have you been?" Walker growled.

"It's Sunday," Ralph said. "You told me I could take the day off to work on the house you owned down by the river, the one Jack and me bought from you." At least Ralph had had the good sense to change from his work clothes to his uniform.

Jack was only moments behind his cousin Ralph. His hair had smudges of blue paint in it. "What's going on, Howard?"

"I wouldn't tell a newspaper editor yet except that Ralph needs to know, and I know how bad he is at keeping his trap shut," Walker complained. "A group of men met here over the weekend to have a private meeting. Turns out it was part of the leadership of the Institute of Divine Intervention upstate. The leader, a man named Charles

Pottinger, who called himself Brother Goodheart, was murdered here overnight."

As a reporter, Jack was delighted. He pulled out the small notebook he was never without and a stub of a pencil and wrote it down. "Found the murderer yet?"

"No. But we're holding the rest of the group until they can be confined at Matteawan, and we have one more from the Institute on the way here to put in with those to be questioned."

"Who would that be?"

"The treasurer of the outfit—the fellow they were plotting to get rid of. Jack, you must keep this under your hat until I know more. The Newburg police have seized all their records and are taking them to Albany. It seems to have to do with money gone missing, possibly on several fronts."

"Wow!" Jack said. "What a deal! This might make you famous, Howard—the guy who pulled the plug on these pious Bible-thumping phonies."

Walker gave Jack a wry look and turned to Ralph. "Harry Harbinger and Robert are keeping three of them on the third floor. You need to take over. And Chief Colling is loaning us another officer and a fingerprint expert. Go upstairs and herd them back into the dining room for luncheon. The outside doors have been locked and Harry has the key. You stay in the dining room with them and I'll let you know when you can turn them loose."

Chapter 9

Lily, Howard Walker, and the Prinneys were having lunch in the kitchen when Robert came in to tell Walker that he had a new bunch of guests: Big Jimmy Rennie, the enormous Deputy Lawrence on loan, and another deputy who was taking the car they'd arrived in back to Chief Colling's station. There was also a tall, thin man with a locked box of fingerprinting materials who introduced himself as Detective Williams.

"May I take them into the dining room?" Walker asked nobody in particular. He stuffed the last of his meat loaf sandwich in his mouth and swigged it down with a gulp of Mrs. Prinney's fake coffee made of chicory.

Everyone nodded vague agreement with his request. As Walker headed into the front entry, he thanked the deputy who was about to leave and directed the other three men to the dining room. Detective Williams took the suspects' fingerprints, including Big Jimmy Rennie's, before he went upstairs to start collecting the same from objects in their rooms.

When Big Jimmy Rennie had been fingerprinted, Walker escorted him to the library. Wiping his hands carefully to get rid of the ink, Rennie took a leisurely look around the room. He cast his glance over the glass-fronted bookshelves, the long, graceful table in the center, and stood, relaxed, by a leather chair next to the French windows that overlooked the magnificent view of the Hudson flowing along below and behind the mansion.

Walker studied the man before sitting down at the table. Considering what he was named, Walker had expected a sloppy man, probably Irish, with a beer belly, red hair, and a florid, blotched face. That would teach him a good lesson in forming impressions of people he hadn't met.

Big Jimmy was smooth. Overconfident. Tall but on the heavy side. Dressed in a pricey, well-fitting suit. Handsome for a man Walker guessed to be around sixty years old. Tanned with white hair, and ever-so-faint scars where he'd had his face hitched up near the front of his well-groomed, old-fashioned sideburns.

Rennie studied the view, nodding with approval. He finally sat down across from Robert. Smiling with big, perfect white teeth that were probably very expensive dentures, he said mildly, "What's this all about, sir?"

"Charles Pottinger's been murdered in his bath here in this house."

"No!" he said, seeming only mildly surprised. "That explains his absence this morning and our having to replay one of his best speeches."

Walker relaxed back into his chair, staring at Rennie and saying nothing. He'd learned that silence with an individual like this was usually the best policy.

"How was he killed?" Rennie asked.

"He was stabbed."

"I presume the others who were missing from the Institute were here with him?"

"Whom do you mean?" Walker asked as if it were only a matter of curiosity.

"Price, Hazard, and Kinsey," he said with a faint smile. "It was awfully quiet up there over the weekend with them missing."

Walker didn't reply. A long silence ensued.

Finally Jimmy Rennie leaned forward and asked, "Why have you brought me here?"

"Why do you think?"

"Because I was the reason for the meeting, I assume."

"That's one of them," Walker said casually.

"What are the other reasons?"

Walker tented his fingers as if deep in thought. He finally said, "Can you account for where you were overnight on Saturday?"

Rennie laughed softly. "I certainly can. I was at home with my wife. We had her brother, his wife, and her niece and nephew to dinner. The brother and sister are twins and it was in honor of their joint birthday. We gave the boy a rather good watch and the girl a long silk scarf."

"And after dinner?" Walker asked.

"A bridge party with a few neighbors invited along."

You are so smooth that you're downright slick, Howard thought.

"And what were you doing at midnight and after?"

"The guests left at eleven. My wife and I said our prayers and went to bed."

"In the same bed?"

"My dear sir, you shock me!" Rennie said, still smiling. "How can that possibly be any of your business?"

Deputy Lawrence, posted at the door, snorted.

"How can it not be?" Walker answered easily.

Rennie looked out the long windows for a moment and, not meeting Walker's eyes, said, "My wife is in somewhat fragile health. The preparations and long evening of socializing had made her tired. I went to the adjoining dressing room and read a bit of a fine book of old sermons for a while. Then I went to check that my wife was sleeping and went to sleep myself in the single bed in the dressing room."

Walker knew Rennie was lying. There probably wasn't even a book of sermons in his house. He knew, too, that Rennie knew he knew it.

Walker rose and said, "That's all I have to ask you now. All the Institute's records are being sent to Albany today. You and your cohorts will shortly be taken to lodge at Matteawan for a few days, where I'll be questioning all of you more thoroughly."

This shook him. "The insane asylum? Have you yourself gone mad?"

"Quite the contrary." Walker rose and went to the door. "Officer Lawrence, stay at the door until I summon you, if you please." He glanced back at Big Jimmy Rennie, who'd gone extraordinarily pale under his tan.

By three o'clock, the asylum had sent their truck. Walker inspected it. The cab was blocked off from the back part with metal and a very small thick glass window. The body of it was sturdy. The truck had no windows except in front, and the back door had three separate locks on it.

Walker had decided to send all the guests to the asylum. He'd considered keeping Edward Price at Grace and Favor and close at hand, but on second thought had decided against it. Price seemed honest and his best source of information about this Institute. But Walker simply didn't like Price and didn't feel he could trust him. Price was obviously now out of work and might disappear. What's more, the Brewsters and Prinneys deserved to be rid of all their guests.

Price was the last to get in the truck and was looking scared to death. Lily and Robert were watching from a window above.

"I know!" Lily exclaimed.

"Know what?"

"Who Edward Price reminds me of. Albert Campion."

"Who is that?"

"Margery Allingham's detective. That's not his real name, of course. He's Rupert and some kind of relative of royalty. But he detects as Albert and acts like a stupid idiot and tricks people out of information to solve the murders."

Robert stared at her for a long moment. "What on earth are you talking about? How do you know these people and who is Margery Allingham? Does she live around here?"

"No, she writes mystery novels."

"You're not talking about real people?"

"They seem real to me. She's a good writer. The first one I read was *The Black Dudley Murder*. And I just finished *Police at the Funeral*. Campion is better in that. Miss Exley ordered it especially for me and let me borrow it first."

"And how do you know Price looks like this fictional Campion?"

"Because Miss Allingham describes him so well, I know exactly what he looks like. But he wears a different kind of glasses. Horn-rimmed, instead of metal. I knew it would come to me eventually."

Robert puffed up dramatically and said, "Lily, you really shouldn't believe everything you read. You're sounding like a thirteen-year-old instead of a grown woman."

Lily said, "I'll lend you *Police at the Funeral*. I still have it in my room. You'll see what I mean. It's not due back at the library for another week."

"I think I better finish reading up on croquet first," Robert said, leaving her watching the truck disappear with its own collection of stupid idiots. And probably at least one real murderer.

Chapter 10

Howard Walker knew this crime wasn't going to be solved very soon. Too much waiting on the people in Albany working over the paperwork. Too much investigation to complete. He'd have to question everyone he'd just sent away in the truck to the asylum much more thoroughly. And he had only three days to do it before most of them would be let out to go their own ways. Reverend Nobby Hazard was the only one loony enough likely to be kept there. Now that the Institute had lost its kingpin, they'd all scatter as fast as they could. He didn't have the staff or the budget or a location to put the suspects under house arrest.

He had to interview Mrs. Rennie about the evening of the murder. He needed to wait for the fingerprint information on the knife and the suspects' belongings and get all the suspects questioned intensively as well. Not that there was much hope of any of them telling the truth.

And he wasn't at all sure he even had all the

suspects locked up. How could he guess how many other people were employed at the Institute of Divine Intervention? And there were outsiders to consider as well.

A man like Pottinger probably had lots of enemies. All fanatics did. And most fanatics hated other fanatics.

The first thing to do was to search all their rooms. They hadn't been allowed to take away their belongings. All of the rooms and their contents were now gray with fingerprinting dust.

He released Harry Harbinger to get back to his life and kept Ralph Summer and Officer Lawrence to help with the search of the rooms. Detective Williams had taken his evidence to Colling's office to examine and compare his data. Jack Summer, the nosy editor, had gone home to change his clothes and come back to snoop around and ask a lot of questions. Most of which Walker refused to answer.

"Jack, I only know there was a murder so far. You can print that and give the name of the victim. That's all. Leave me alone to learn more about it before you nag me."

"I have a newspaper to get out this week," Jack objected. "This is too big a story to ignore. Brother Goodheart is a national celebrity. I'll sell a ton of papers by getting the first shot at this story, and other papers clear across the country will want permission to reprint."

"I'll tell you whatever I'm allowed to when I

know more," Walker said. "Now, get out of here and let me get on with my job."

"Can't I just watch you search the rooms?"

"No. Go away."

Detective Williams had been the first to have information, and it was negative.

"No prints on the bathtub. Not even Pottinger's. There's a towel on the floor somebody used to wipe them all off. Towels don't take prints," he said as if Walker needed to be told this. "I'll call your office when I know more."

Walker started the search in Pottinger's suite. The man had made very few notes. His small suitcase contained only his cheap wig and a couple of changes of underwear. His toothbrush and tooth powder can was on the edge of the sink with his shaving materials. There was also another five hundred dollars in the suitcase with a gold clip holding the bills and a note saying "for the end of the meeting."

That money would have to be sorted out eventually. Presumably Pottinger had meant to use it to pay the Brewsters at the end of their visit, but possibly it was meant to pay off the other men he was conspiring with.

There were no other documents except an address book in Pottinger's suit jacket with the list of employees at the Institute, many of them crossed out.

Walker found this interesting as he flipped through the pages. Pottinger seemed to have a lot of turnover, especially among the few women who worked as secretaries. He wondered how many of them were still at the addresses he had for them. Probably not many. Some of the entries had been crossed out so thoroughly that the paper was dented.

Why, he wondered, did so many of them leave? How would he find any of them?

He didn't even know if Pottinger had ever married. He knew very little about the man except that he appeared to make a great deal of money on his preaching. Walker had only accidentally heard some of his talks when someone else was listening to them on the radio in the living room at his boarding house, and he had deliberately tuned them out. He didn't enjoy programs that had so much yelling, bigotry, and pontificating. Fibber McGee was more fun to listen to.

Had all these women left their jobs voluntarily? Was Pottinger a womanizer? It wouldn't surprise him. At this point, nothing about the man would surprise him. Maybe the opposite was true: that he disliked having women on the staff, but occasionally had to put up with them, then discarded them as soon as he could.

Walker and Officer Lawrence carefully searched the rest of the room, looking under furniture, turning out the seemingly unused bed, picking up the few ornaments set over the fireplace to see if there was anything pertinent under them, turning over pictures on the walls.

"It's odd, isn't it," Walker said to Officer Lawrence, "that nobody appears to have made notes about the meeting."

"Maybe they did and that other fellow who stayed in the back room flushed or burned them."

Then they went to the room where Edward Price had stayed, at the end of the narrow hall past the bathroom. Edward was the secretary, so he must have taken notes. They found his pad of papers under the unmade bed.

It was mainly a list of meal times, arrival times, and prayer times, which explained the mysterious chanting that Lily told him Phoebe Twinkle had reported. The rest of the notes were in shorthand. Walker knew Lily had been studying shorthand, but not for long enough to know it well. He showed it to Officer Lawrence. "Do you know shorthand?"

"Yes, sir."

"Take a look at this and tell me what it says."

Lawrence glanced through and said, "I can't make sense of it, I'm afraid. Everybody's shorthand becomes personal to them after they've done it for a long time. You'll probably have to send the notebook to Albany as well and let them find someone who knows more about the variations."

Walker ran his hands through his hair. By the time this was done, all his suspects would have flown away to the four winds. This was a case he feared would never be solved and would become a huge blot on his good reputation.

They moved on next to Nobby Hazard's room. It stank of his hair oil, and a huge bottle of it was on the windowsill. There was no label on it; apparently it was a noxious recipe he mixed himself. Other than his suitcase and his shaving materials, this was the only item in the room. Nobby apparently had no use for tooth care. Walker opened the small, battered case. Nobby had two changes of underwear, one extra shirt. The clothes were all old and stained and looked as if they'd been with him for decades, being fruitlessly washed and ironed and darned. The extra shirt had been meticulously patched at the elbows, collar, and cuffs. Did he do this sewing himself, or did he have some downtrodden wife or spinster daughter in the background?

There were two books in the suitcase. One was an old Bible. The fake leather cover had crumbled to bits. The spine was a wreck. Almost every page had a smudge on the lower outer corner. Nobby must have gone through it hundreds of times, wetting his finger to turn the pages, many of which had come loose from the binding. Nearly the whole of Revelations was unhinged.

Naturally that would be Nobby's favorite section. There was a great deal of precise underlining throughout.

With distaste, Walker stuffed Revelations back in place as best as he could and put the Bible back in the case and picked up the other book. It turned out to be an equally battered expanding file folder instead of a book, stuffed with receipts, business cards, notes of dates, and costs of hotels, drivers, train tickets, meals, drinks, and room service charges.

Noticeably absent were notations about cash coming in from Brother Goodheart's preaching. It seemed that Nobby never knew how much was made on these many trips, though he knew precisely what was spent and how. Walker would send this along to Albany as well.

He was still convinced this murder was all about money. But someone had killed the fatted calf and put all of them out of business. Who had the motive for this? Where would Nobby, for example, get a new job? With his looks, smell, age, and personality, he'd be unemployable. Price would be out of what must have been an unpleasant but moderately lucrative job. Rennie would lose his access to the cash, and if the conspiracy theory was right and the accountants at Albany could prove it, he'd be in jail.

Walker told himself there was no point in debating this with himself yet until he had a lot more hard information. He took his assistants to the last room occupied by the Institute's guests, the room of attorney Jackson Kinsey.

Kinsey had a large, expensive suitcase full of clothing and law books. Bits of paper bristled at the top of many pages. Walker and Officer Lawrence went through them while Ralph Summer slouched against the door picking his teeth with a penknife.

Walker went through the largest of the four law books, while Officer Lawrence went through another. "What are you finding on those marked pages?" Walker asked.

"Stuff about libel and slander," Lawrence replied.

"Me, too," Walker said. "And here's one about by-laws and the duties and restrictions of treasurers."

They set the books aside and went carefully through the rest of the items in the suitcase. There was nothing remarkable, and here, too, there were no signs of notes made during the meeting. But all of Kinsey's personal belongings were of the best quality. The shirts and underwear were hand-tailored. The extra silk tie must have cost what an average person made in a year. Even his shaving materials were encased in an exotic leather case, and the razor had an ivory handle. So did his hairbrush.

Walker sighed. "Ralph, you can go back to working on the house. Lawrence, will you come with me to the asylum and take notes? We have a lot more things to ask these men about."

Chapter 11

The sense of relief among the residents of Grace and Favor when all the guests and police had left was almost overwhelming. Mimi, the maid, was the only one upset, because Chief Walker had ordered her not to start tidying up any of the rooms on the second and third floors. Mimi, naturally, was itching to take the bedding and start washing it and to get on with the sweeping and mopping of the floors and the beeswaxing of the furniture. She had to content herself with ruthlessly polishing the silver, which didn't need polishing.

Mrs. Prinney was happy that she didn't have to cook for so many extra people anymore, as she was almost out of food. She still had enough meat loaf, bread, and late-season spinach for a dinner, and that's all she needed until Monday, when the greengrocer was in his shop.

Lily, Robert, and Phoebe all retreated to late-afternoon naps. Only Mr. Prinney had too much on his mind to rest. He was still in his office at home, making notes of what could or might be

done about Mary Towerton's husband. Some of
his suggestions to himself were absurd. Especially the one about taking the train out to Hoover
Dam to sort through the mix-up. He felt certain
that her husband was, indeed, dead and the
telegram was simply a spelling error. Otherwise,
how would the people in Arizona have known
her address? Still, he had to have proof for her.

He'd taken a liking to Mrs. Towerton. He felt
unusually fatherly toward her. He admired her
for finding a job niche that was exclusive to her
talents. He also feared that it was possible that
they'd never figure out whether she was wife or
widow. And he hated failing anyone.

He was interrupted by Jack Summer calling on
him just before dinnertime.

"Somebody in town told me they'd seen Mrs.
Towerton coming up the road with her cart to
Grace and Favor. Was she here to see you?" Jack
asked.

"You know perfectly well I can't tell you that."

"I do know. But I care about her. We shared an
awful experience last·summer at the Bonus
March in Washington. We were together in the
thick of the violence, and while we were escaping, her grandfather died in the back of her
wagon. I'm concerned about her welfare. If she's
in some kind of trouble, I'd like to help if I could."

Mr. Prinney thought for a long moment. "There
is something you might be able to tell me. Could
you find out through your sources how many

men are working on that dam out west? All I
know about the project is that there are rumors
that the powers that be are disguising accidents
as illnesses, and I don't even know if that's true."

"Hoover Dam? I'll see if I can find out. I've
saved all the *New York Times* articles and things
from other newspapers for reference. I think I saw
several articles about it. I noticed because Mrs.
Towerton's husband is presumably working
there. I'll copy everything I can find. I don't suppose you could tell me anything about Brother
Goodheart's death? That's going to be a big local
interest and national as well."

"I've deliberately avoided knowing much
about it. You'll have to talk to Chief Walker."

"He's clammed up on me," Jack said.

"As well he should," Mr. Prinney said.

First thing Monday morning, most of the people
at Grace and Favor scattered. Lily went to the
grade school. Mr. Prinney took the photograph of
Mary Towerton and her husband to Poughkeepsie. Mrs. Prinney stocked up on food. Phoebe delivered three altered dresses to customers. Robert
headed for the library, ostensibly to get more
books about games for the children, but really
trying, and failing, to screw up his courage to invite Miss Exley to the films.

Jack Summer put out a special edition of the
newspaper citing what little he knew about
Brother Goodheart's death. It was only a single

page, but he made sure it went to every other newspaper and wire service he could think of.

Howard Walker was out of town as well. He went to the asylum to conduct more interviews with his primary suspects. He'd seen the building a number of times, but not up close. It was the ugliest structure he'd ever seen. And it smelled horrific inside. The odors of stale food, urine, and despair permeated it. And the screams and cries he heard at every turn would haunt him for years.

He came away depressed and discouraged. Nobody would admit to any further knowledge. Nearly the only thing he accomplished was to ask Edward Price if anyone else took notes of the meeting.

"Nobby's next thing to illiterate and Kinsey wouldn't dream of putting anything on paper that someone else might read," Price said.

"Didn't Pottinger have written material ready? Didn't he jot down people's ideas for dealing with Big Jimmy Rennie?"

"Not that I ever saw," Price said.

"One more question," Walker said. "In Pottinger's belongings, there was a wad of money and a note saying it was for the end of the meeting. Did that mean a payoff for you and the others figuring out how to get Rennie in hot water, or was it for the Brewsters?"

Price almost laughed. "We were required to sort out about Rennie as part of our jobs—there was no payment for it. Of course, we never came around to a conclusion. Give it to the Brewsters. Pottinger told me I was to pay it to them as we left."

That afternoon when Chief Walker returned to his office at the boardinghouse, he received a phone call from an accountant in Albany.

"I've been handed the mess of paperwork and it's going to take me quite a while to sort it out. But I've glanced over the treasurer's first."

"What's your opinion at this point?" Walker asked.

The man said, "He's either fully incompetent with bookkeeping or so clever at it that he knows exactly how to fake the incompetence. I'll keep in touch with you as I go along. I just wanted to warn you that it's going to take at least a couple weeks, if not a month or more."

"By that time, he'll be long gone," Walker said.

"I'm afraid so. Sorry for the bad news. I'll do my best for you."

The next call was from Detective Williams, the fingerprint expert. "I've found nothing out of the way. The fingerprints on that big table in the suite tell me who sat where. Other than that, everybody's belongings had only their own fingerprints. There are small fingerprints all over everything in the house."

"Those will be Mimi's. She's the housemaid," Walker said.

"I'll keep all of them just in case they become relevant," Detective Williams said, ringing off.

* * *

Lily discovered that the children were all wound up that Monday morning. They were passing around some secret, she suspected. Bob, the boy who drove his father's truck, seemed to be the source of whatever the gossip was about. Lily debated with herself as to whether she should do some eavesdropping or openly pry it out of the children.

In the end, she decided it was probably something trivial and she was better off not knowing about it. She was there to teach them worthwhile skills, not to pry into their private lives.

She herself was fairly nervous, as well. Tomorrow was Election Day. Would Governor Roosevelt win the presidency? The signs all looked as if he would, but she didn't trust signs, or newspaper and radio speculation. What would happen to the country if by some freak chance Hoover was reelected? Would the government go belly-up? Would there be a true second civil war tearing up the country? Would the middle of the country, the farmers who were hit so hard, try to form their own country as the South had once done? Would the Communists step in and wreck America with Russian rules? They'd been looking for an opportunity to stage a full-fledged revolution.

Could these things happen if Hoover won? She felt sure they could.

Robert, taking over for Lily after lunch, was

wondering the same thing. He didn't even notice the children whispering to each other. He gave a rousing speech to them about reminding their parents to go vote the next day. He was careful not to tell them their parents had to vote for the New York governor, much as he wished to say it. He didn't think Mrs. Tarkington would approve of him doing that.

It was clearly too cold that day to play croquet outside, so he took them to the now empty lunchroom and moved the tables aside to create a tiny croquet court on the floor, with colored paper indicating the wickets. Today he was too worried about the election the next day to even chide them for their rampant cheating and deliberately silly questions.

Robert hadn't voted in the last election, though he had been of age to do so. He knew Lily hadn't either. He couldn't remember if she'd been too young or simply as disinterested as he was.

The last election was while they were still rich and, looking back, extremely simple-minded about politics. About real life, in fact. But if he had voted, the last time, he'd have voted for Hoover. The family had been staunch Republicans, and his father had told them that the man was a famous benefactor. Hoover had seen to it that the starving nations who'd lost their farms and homes in Europe were fed after the Great War.

Hoover had sounded like a nice, compassionate man. Then. Now most of the people in his own country were starving, as Lily and he would have been if Great-uncle Horatio hadn't left them Grace and Favor. This fact, if nothing else was wrong with the President, made Robert nearly rabid.

He'd vote first thing tomorrow. Not that he even knew how or where. As he noticed Mrs. Tarkington going past the door of the lunchroom, he asked where the town voted.

"At the City Hall, on the green. I wonder what sort of turnout there will be. I'm going the moment they open."

When he was finished with the children that afternoon, and after reminding them again to urge their parents to vote, he went home and ran into Lily helping Mrs. Prinney prepare for dinner. "We vote at the City Hall," he said. "Mrs. Tarkington said she was going there when it opened. You might want to as well."

"I'd have to get up at the crack of dawn to stand in line and vote before school starts," Lily said. "I think I'll wait till the afternoon. And I can drop in on Phoebe and make sure she's voted, too."

"Right. Hey, Lily, how about if I spend the morning swanning around the countryside in the Duesie bringing people in to vote?"

"That's a grand idea," Lily said. "Everybody would love to ride in it. And you better find Howard Walker and remind him to take time out to vote, as well. I think he's spending today again at the asylum, questioning those awful people he so nicely removed from Grace and Favor."

"I'm not going to the asylum for him. Imagine the people who might want to come along for the ride!"

Chapter 12

Bright and early on Election Day, Robert appealed to Mrs. Prinney. "I need a banner for the Duesie."

"How big?" Mrs. Prinney asked calmly. She'd become very mellow now that the guests were gone.

"As big as we can do. I want it to say, 'Free Ride to Vote for Roosevelt.' "

"Give me fifteen minutes," the older woman said.

She turned up with ten feet of old muslin. "Will this do?"

"Brilliantly. I found some red paint in the garage. How do I get the banner on the car?"

"Thin the paint so it will dry fast and I'll see what I can do." She fired up the kitchen stove and as soon as Robert had the banner done, they hung it from a clothesline she'd rigged up across the room.

"That should only take a little time. Now let's look over the car."

Robert already had the Duesie parked at the front door. They found various places they could tie it onto the driver's side of the vehicle. By the time they'd figured it out, the paint was dry and stinking up the house. "It's a wonder it didn't blow up and burn the mansion down," Robert said. "Thank you so much!"

He was moved to give Mrs. Prinney a kiss on her cheek, then got in the car and roared off, leaving her in the driveway, blushing.

Her husband discovered her standing outside a moment later. "Emmaline, you don't even have a coat on. What are you doing? Come inside and bundle up. We need to go vote."

After Mrs. Prinney had changed from her housedress to a decent public dress, her best hat, coat, stockings, shoes, and her most flattering corset, they drove to town.

Meanwhile, Robert was driving the country roads, honking for people to come out and take a ride. Soon the Duesie was loaded to the gills with farmers, their wives, and whatever voting-age children they could round up. Muddy boots and trousers were the order of the day, but Robert, for once, didn't care. He could clean it up later.

He dropped off his cargo at City Hall, calling to them, "I'll be back in half an hour to pick you up," and sped off to collect a new group on another road.

By noon, when he was to be at the school, he figured he'd hauled more than forty voters to the polls. He dropped the last group off at their homes and went to ask Lily if she could handle one more hour so he could get at least ten or twelve more. She came out of the lunchroom and gasped. The banner was impressive, but the car was filthy.

"How will you ever get it cleaned?"

"I'll manage somehow. I might have to drive it into the front hall so I don't freeze my hands mopping it up."

"Robert, listen. I'll take all your afternoon classes for you on one condition."

"What's that?"

"That before you take me home, you give the kids in our class a ride and take me to vote. I kept watching for the line to become shorter all morning, and thanks to you, it never did."

Virtually the whole juvenile population of the school was pooling around the car like a bunch of curious fish, touching the finish, oohing and aahing over the dirty leather upholstery. Two of the boys had already crawled under it to look at the gears. Lily warned Robert of this and called the children back inside, checking one last time that nobody was still under the Duesie before Robert drove off.

By three-thirty he was back and had loaded up Lily and the boys and girls to take them home in style. By this time Robert himself was as dirty as the car, and the children seemed to absorb a lot of the dirt on the way.

"Their mothers are going to have fits when they see them," Lily said.

"Most of their mothers have ridden in it already, and some of them brought along the mess themselves. Roxanne Anderson had been canning fruit she dried over the summer for pies. She smeared sticky juice all over the dashboard," Robert said. "I've tried to keep count. I think I rounded up over sixty voters by the time I lost track."

Lily could hardly hear him for the delighted squeals of the children. He stopped to let her vote, insisting that Lily go to the head of the long line in honor of his contribution to rounding up voters, and had a hard time keeping the children in the car.

Lily was tired by the time he dropped her off, and she had some of Mrs. Anderson's pie filling on her coat sleeve. Robert kept going, trying to find more voters before the polls closed. Lily cleaned up her coat and took a quick bath.

By seven-thirty, Robert was home. He was filthy and exhausted, but jubilant.

"I did my part to elect the president. Who would have thought I'd have come to this? I even managed to vote. And I scooped up Howard Walker and made him vote, cranky as he was."

For the only time in their history at Grace and Favor, the residents of the house ate their dinner with the radio on. The early returns were starting to come in and sounded good. But most of them were from the northeastern states, where Roosevelt was well known. It would be hours before the Midwest would report and even later for the West Coast. Robert was driving them all so crazy gabbing on about his contribution and his tallies that they told him to go take a nap.

Phoebe decided at ten to give up listening, and the Prinneys were nodding off in their chairs by eleven, when Robert came back downstairs with sleep-tousled hair. "Have you kept up my tally?" he demanded of Lily.

"Of course I have. Take a look."

By midnight it was clear that Governor Roosevelt had won the presidency by an enormous landslide. Lily was thrilled, but Robert pointed out that no matter how grand this was, Roosevelt wouldn't take office for another five months.

"Hoover knows he's out now. He has no incentive left to care about the country. Five months is enough to get a revolution going."

"I don't think it will happen," Lily said, meaning she hoped it wouldn't.

"Maybe you're right. Now that the voters have spoken loud and clear, they'll be willing to wait for better times. Lily, could you take my half day of teaching again tomorrow so I can clean the car?"

"Absolutely not. You're the one who had the nap."

"I'd trade you two whole days."

"No. Miss Langston might be back before you can do it."

"I'll do it this week. I promise."

"Oh, all right. I'm going to bed now. I won't forget the promise."

"I can cope with grammar, but you know I'm at sea with arithmetic," Robert waffled.

"They can go two days without arithmetic then. I haven't time to teach you anything you can teach them. We'll just reverse what we already teach to the other half of the day."

Robert looked confused.

"You know what I mean," Lily said. "I'm just too tired to say it right. *Good night*, Robert."

Howard Walker couldn't stand waiting for information to come to him, so on Wednesday he went hunting for anything he could find out about his suspects. He called nearly every law enforcement person he was acquainted with. All of them knew about Brother Goodheart, and one had interesting information.

"We went after him when I was starting out as a cop in Nebraska. That's where he was born, around 1885. Regularly beat by his father. He did time for petty larceny when he held up the town pharmacy. That's when I caught him. Then he did time again after that for attacking a young woman in the town. Went east, about the same time I did, working his way along as a traveling preacher. I've kept my eye on him for a long time, hoping to catch him out at something else, but it seems someone's bumped him off, from what you say."

"Would you care to guess who?" Walker asked the retired chief of police of Kingston, a town upstate.

"Either someone he was stealing from or a woman who was brave enough to complain about being fondled against her will. Not much help, I'm afraid. But I have a little time on my hands. Let me see if I can find anything more about him up here. If so, I'll call you back."

Walker wasn't surprised about Pottinger's background and found himself thinking about the address book of Brother Goodheart's with so many secretaries' names crossed out. Maybe his murder had to do with money being stolen, but the women were a possibility as well. Howard couldn't imagine that Goodheart was very appealing to women, except the hand-picked converts to his religious fervor whom he'd paraded as beneficiaries of his generosity at public meetings.

The next old friend he contacted confirmed that Goodheart's attorney, Jackson Kinsey, had been disbarred in Vermont, as Edward Price had indicated.

"What for?" Walker asked.

"Bigamy, as I recall. And something else I've forgotten. Oh, yes. Something about stealing money from a trust he was handling and the grown children took him to court and won a big settlement. I knew I'd think of it."

This only served to confirm that Edward Price was indeed a reliable source of information. Regarding Kinsey, at least. Walker wondered what else Price knew that he had withheld. Perhaps about himself.

Chief Walker drove back to the asylum and found out first that the director there was thinking of holding Nobby Hazard longer and considering keeping him. He was proving to be quite a loud and offensive customer, and they were looking into his history to see if he had a criminal record.

Walker hoped they'd find some reason to lock Nobby up for a good long time. He asked to see Edward Price out on the grounds for privacy's sake.

Price had suffered from his incarceration. "I want out of this place! I'm not a loony or a criminal!" he exclaimed, close to tears of frustration. "You have no idea what goes on here. People screaming all night. I've had about five hours of sleep since I arrived here. The stench is unbelievable. And they've sent me out to the gardens to muck around in the dirt. I'm not an outdoor person, and I don't even have a warm coat."

Walker listened and somewhat sympathized, but wasn't about to release Price until he had to. He showed him Goodheart's address book. "Why are so many women's names crossed out?"

"Because he was a lecherous man. Isn't it obvious?"

"Do you know where any of these women have gone?"

"How would I know? I had very little to do with any of them except to give them things to type up. And I don't think all of them were secretaries anyway. They might have been the teachers at the orphanage."

"Orphanage? There was an orphanage at the Institute? Nobody's mentioned this before."

Price ran his hand through his dirty hair. "A working orphanage. The kids lived in a little place that was a former barn. Not even heated, except for a woodstove Mrs. Rennie contributed."

"Big Jimmy's wife?"

"She's a nice woman. The real point of the thing was slave labor. The children were assigned to make the collection baskets that were later sold after the money was collected. Poor little things. But Mrs. Rennie stepped in again and made Goodheart hire two women to teach them basic skills. Reading and writing and arithmetic. Just enough to possibly get them jobs when they grew up. Every now and then they had a bath and brush-up and were allowed to wear nice clothes to be shown off at preaching meetings."

Price sat silent for a long moment. "I know it'll make you suspect me when you shouldn't, but I can't help saying that Goodheart was a real bastard."

Chapter 13

While he still had Big Jimmy Rennie confined, Chief Walker decided to have a talk with Rennie's wife.

He found the address to be a large, well-kept house on the west side of the Hudson, with a nice view of the river. It wasn't as close to the Institute as he'd supposed it would be. Apparently Rennie kept a decent space between his work and his home. A maid answered his knock.

"I'm Chief of Police Howard Walker. I need to speak to Mrs. Rennie."

The maid looked shocked.

"She has nothing to fear from me. I just need a bit of information," he said.

Mrs. Rennie appeared moments later. She was a lovely though frail looking woman of about sixty in a very nice black-and-white polka-dot dress. She moved as if it were painful to do so.

Having gained entrance, he introduced himself properly. "I'm Chief of Police Howard Walker, Mrs. Rennie."

She paled. "Are you the man holding my husband in that awful place?"

"I'm afraid I am. But I had to hold him along with those who were present when Brother Goodheart was murdered. I'd like to ask you a few questions."

"I don't think I should be speaking with you."

"My questions are unofficial. I'm not taking notes. And I'm not asking about your husband."

"What are you asking then?" she said, unwillingly ushering him to the living room. Like the hallway, this room was elegant and generously proportioned. The parquet floor was partially covered by a few beautiful Oriental rugs, a fire burned in the large white marble fireplace, and there was plenty of comfortable seating. Expensive-looking works of art hung on the wall, and there were a half a dozen tastefully framed family pictures on the grand piano. Someone, probably this woman, had very good taste. It was the sort of house Walker would have liked to live in someday.

"I want to speak with you about Brother Goodheart. Or more accurately, Charles Pottinger. I understood from something that was said to me that you took something of an interest in the orphans at the Institute."

"Poor little things," she said. "They were mostly children of migrant families who couldn't afford to take care of them and abandoned them. They should have been adopted out instead of being at the Institute."

"I take it you're no longer involved with this, since you're using the past tense. Or do you mean they are no longer there?"

"I presume the children are still there. But it broke my heart to see them, and I couldn't keep going there without saying something that my husband wouldn't have approved of. I knew he would agree with me but not like hearing it from me. The children were treated as slaves."

"Whose fault was that? Who was supposed to care for them?"

She looked at him with pity. "Brother Good-heart, of course. It was all his own idea. They were simple showpieces. But he seemed to feel they had to pay for the privilege."

"You didn't like him?"

She gave a long sigh, the sigh of a woman about to pour out her heart. "I loathed him. He was preaching simply for money. He should have called himself Brother Evilheart. Have you ever listened to him on the radio?"

"Not willingly," Walker admitted.

"He was a bigot," she said, her thin, pale face flushing. "He was always praising Herr Hitler for his wisdom. He went on and on about how the Jews, especially the greedy Jewish bankers of the world, were responsible for the state of our country. I suppose he believed this before the Crash. That gave him a cause and a downtrodden audience who needed to place blame on someone other than Hoover or themselves."

She'd obviously given this a lot of thought, and probably never could tell anyone else how she felt, Howard thought. He was glad she'd revealed her thoughts to him. She'd probably been bursting with views she had to be very careful to conceal.

"These people he preached at were the poorest of all," she went on. "He was perfectly happy to take their pitiful savings. And in case you're wondering"—she made a gesture that included her large, well-furnished house—"this was my parents' house. I owned it before I was even married. If you're holding my husband because you think he was part of the theft, you're wrong."

"Have you visited him at the asylum?"

"No, he said it was a place he hoped I'd never have to see. He's very protective of me. He managed to talk someone into letting him use their telephone. He told me you'd seized all his financial records."

"I had to. You must know that," Walker said. "There's an enormous amount of money at stake. That's why Pottinger and his cronies were meeting in secret."

He probably shouldn't have told her this, except that her husband clearly must have known. He'd probably already passed the information along to her, or she wouldn't have told Walker she'd inherited this house.

"Regarding Goodheart," he went on, "was his attitude real? Or do you think it was put on just to draw the crowds?"

"Oh, it was real enough. He never privately admitted he did it for the money. He believed, God help him, that he was right. And being right, it entitled him to live, as they say, 'high on the hog.' The best hotels. The most expensive food, drink, and women."

Walker nodded and then asked, "I trust your judgment. What about Nobby Hazard?"

Mrs. Rennie merely shuddered at the sound of the name. There was no need to speak.

"Jackson Kinsey?"

She sighed. "You're probably thinking I'm a vicious gossip. Mr. Kinsey is an outright crook. The only one there besides my husband who seemed a decent person is that young man Edward Price. I suspect he hates his job, but he's never said so outright. He was upset about the orphans as well. It's the only criticism I've heard from him. Of course, a few of the teachers and secretaries sometimes made complaints, but I never knew many of the secretaries. I seldom went to the big building, just the farmhouse where the orphans were."

She started to silently cry, tears running down her face as if she were unaware of it. "I've begged my husband more than once to get another job."

"What did he say?" Walker asked, violating his promise not to ask about Big Jimmy.

Apparently Mrs. Rennie had forgotten his promise as well.

"He said he was too proud to live on my inheritance. Good jobs are hard to find these days hereabouts, and he didn't want me to have to leave this house. He knows how much I love it. I tried to convince him that since we had no children of our own, we might as well live on my money instead of his income alone. He wouldn't hear of it."

Walker was reluctantly considering changing his opinion of Big Jimmy. Maybe the accountant in Albany was right that he was simply incompetent rather than crooked. If his wife wasn't seriously misjudging him, he was apparently a good, honorable husband, at the least.

"Of course, he's going to have to consider it now," Mrs. Rennie said sadly. "Pottinger was the kingpin of the Institute and now he's dead. What will become of the orphans now?"

Walker had no answer to the question.

Chapter 14

Life for most of the residents of Voorburg-on-Hudson should have gone back to normal for the rest of the week. Chief Walker's prime suspects were released from the Asylum for the Criminally Insane late Wednesday evening, all except Nobby Hazard, who was kept because he appeared to be a true lunatic, if not a downright criminal. The director, who loved working with religious obsessives, was still checking him out in several states to see if he had a criminal record.

Walker doubted that his main suspect, the treasurer, Big Jimmy Rennie, would disappear when he was released. At least he wouldn't if his wife was correct in her assessment of his devotion to her and knowing how much she loved her lifelong home.

Edward Price had reported in to Walker that he'd gone to stay with his sister in Hyde Park while looking for a new job. He'd given Walker her name and address.

Walker also assumed the attorney for the Institute was probably so entrenched in his home and private office that he wouldn't be able to pull up sticks immediately. All Walker could accomplish was to continue to interview the few people remaining at the Institute. He would try to find out where the women who were listed in Pottinger's address book had gone while he waited for word from Albany.

A new problem suddenly emerged. Lily had already expressed fear to Robert that when Jack Summer had sent out his announcement of Brother Goodheart's murder at a mansion in Voorburg, they'd be inundated with reporters from all over the country. But it hadn't happened.

Until now.

The reporters had been busy covering the national election. However, when it was determined that Roosevelt had won, they turned their full attention to Voorburg and Brother Goodheart's death. They'd started out at the Institute of Divine Intervention first, arriving in droves early Wednesday morning.

Chief Colling had had to insist that doors all be locked and had tried his best to drive the reporters away.

"There's nobody here," Colling told them. "Just one secretary and Goodheart's attorney winding up his estate. And you know a lawyer's not going to talk to you or let the secretary do so either." He didn't bother mentioning the orphans or the teacher in the converted barn.

Balked of their main source of information, it took them very little time to find out from the citizens of Voorburg which mansion was the site of the murder.

Their invasion was what finally convinced Mr. Prinney that Grace and Favor needed locks. Several of the mob camped out in the cold had already discovered that not all the doors had locks. They'd found their way into the house by nine-thirty in the morning and scared Mimi, Lily, and Mrs. Prinney half to death asking if they'd seen the body.

Was there lots of blood? Who else was staying there? What were all the names of the actual residents of the place? Were they devotees of the notorious preacher? Had one of them killed the man?

Howard Walker had to get rid of them. The house was searched thoroughly. One reporter was located in the master suite bathroom trying to convince Mimi to stage a reenactment of the crime. Mimi had slapped him for even suggesting this. Another was found under Edward Price's bed trying to find clues.

When they were all removed from the interior, the reporters took over the guest house that once guarded the entrance. They brought in dead wood to make a fire with and very nearly burned it down.

Walker went to Robert and said, "Go down in the basement and bring up the oldest, best bottle of whiskey down there."

When Robert had done so, Walker went to the guest house and sat down, with the dusty old bottle prominently displayed in his lap. He wiped the dust away from the label.

"Boys, here's the situation," he said, fondling the bottle carelessly so the label was facing the reporters. "There's nobody here who knows anything. Goodheart didn't tell them who he was. He didn't introduce anyone. They took food up to them and left it outside the door. There's only a brother and sister who are local teachers, a cook, her husband, and a widow woman who's the maid."

He didn't think Mimi would like being described this way, but he wanted to suggest an old and possibly dotty retainer.

"There's nothing you can learn here." He set the bottle of whiskey on a table and said, "I'll be back in half an hour. I want all of you and the bottle to be gone by then."

"Thank heaven they didn't know about the previous death that took place here," Robert said, watching as the reporters drifted away, passing the bottle around. "We don't want to become celebrities that way."

But there was worse to come.

Most of the reporters had already called in stories about Brother Goodheart's murder, embroidering it with what little they knew or could get away with saying. When the news was out, mobs of

Goodheart's faithful made a pilgrimage to the Institute, wanting to see "the Divine Body," as they'd taken to calling the corpse. They wanted to know where he was to be buried so they could contribute to a wonderful edifice for his eternal rest.

Chief Colling dealt with them as well. "He's already on his way back to Nebraska to be interred where he was born. There's no one here."

The truth was Colling had no idea where Goodheart was buried and didn't care.

When the first wave left, he put a big notice on the front door saying the same thing to those who were bound to arrive later from farther away. His notice mentioned that nobody was in the building and that all the doors were locked and guarded by the police. Which wasn't true either.

He called Chief Walker and warned him that the devout adherents of Brother Goodheart, while blinded to his faults, weren't all entirely stupid. Like the reporters, they would soon find out where he'd been murdered. They were bound to figure out where Grace and Favor was located.

Whiskey wasn't appropriate this time. Walker wrote out a statement that the residents of the mansion didn't know anything about the death of Brother Goodheart. In fact, they hadn't even known the identity of the guests who were staying at their home.

He also arranged for Ralph Summer, Harry Harbinger, and himself to go on twenty-four-hour rotation, if it became necessary, to read the statement to the hordes who were bound to be appearing at the door.

After the bulk of them had been turned away, he'd left the notice on the front and back doors. He told the Prinneys and Brewsters to leave all the lights off in the rooms in front of the house for at least a week and be careful not to be seen coming and going from the mansion.

There was a path from the kitchen door to the barn where the Duesie was concealed. Strangers wouldn't know about it, so the residents should take this route when they left or came home.

Mr. Prinney broke down and asked Walker's advice about a good locksmith.

Robert kept his promise to Lily about taking her duties in return for letting him off the hook Election Day. Both of them were enjoying instructing the children, so long as it was only half days for each.

"They wear me out by noon," Lily said. "I'm not used to such young people with so much spare energy. I'd be a candidate for the asylum as well as our former guests if I had to do it all day."

Walker and his assistants had finally finished examining the rooms and belongings of the guests at Grace and Favor, and normalcy resumed at the mansion as well. Mimi cleaned as if she were demented. Everyone was happy, except for Mr. Prinney, who hadn't heard back from Jack

Summer yet and was getting anxious to help Mary Towerton.

He dropped in the newspaper office on Thursday afternoon to check with the editor and found Jack nearly buried in snippets of paperwork, fresh new file folders, and a beat-up third- or fourth-hand file cabinet he'd found at the city dump.

"I'm sorry it's taken me so long. The mob of reporters is harassing me for inside stuff I don't know anything about. Their pestering ate up my time," Jack said. "And I had much more material about Hoover Dam than I realized. You can't take the time to sort through all of this, but I'll have a summary ready for you tomorrow."

Mr. Prinney had to be satisfied with this. Looking around at the wealth of various files and articles, he realized Jack was right.

Jack dutifully turned up at Mr. Prinney's office early Friday and said, "I've made sort of a summary for you. It's comprehensive, but if there's anything else you need to know about it, I have it sorted out chronologically now."

Jack was prepared to give Prinney his notes, but wanted to read them aloud to him first. Perhaps Mr. Prinney might just happen to say something revealing. Jack assumed this had something to do with Mary Towerton, who was, so far as he knew, the only person in Voorburg who had a personal connection with the Hoover Dam.

"The plan has been going on for years. The Colorado River, I believe, is the one that carved out the Grand Canyon," he began. "At the border of Nevada and Arizona, the river also carved out a deep canyon. At the turn of the century, a government agency decided to divert some of the water by canals to the southern California deserts. This was great for the farmers, until a few years later when it flooded the area so badly it created an enormous lake of red mud and wrecked their farms and homes."

Jack turned a page and went on, "Then in 1920 the same idea came under consideration again by the Bureau of Reclamation with a plan for damming it and sending the water to lots of people. In 1922, President Hoover, who was then Secretary of Commerce, got wind of it. As an engineer himself, he liked the idea. But the government didn't like the price. It wasn't until 1929 that the funding was approved. Apparently there was some kind of very expensive bond that had to be posted by the people who would do the work, and it took a lot of time to get the money."

Mr. Prinney was interested, but waiting for the information he needed. "Yes, go on."

"It was too huge a job for any one company to take on," Jack said, flipping to the next page of his notes. "So several groups of companies with the necessary skills and reputations formed something called 'Six Companies.' Some of them are experienced demolition experts; others are concrete experts. One is a road-building company. I don't know what the others are. Anyway, they hired a guy named Frank Crowe to oversee the whole thing. He had the reputation of being the best civil engineer in the country."

"Is this gentleman still in charge?" Mr. Prinney asked.

"Yes, he is. And he's doing a great job as far as the schedule goes. He's way ahead of his deadlines, but he's working the men too hard and not taking the necessary precautions. A number of the thousands of men working there have died. The rumor you said you heard was right. A few accidents have been reported, but mainly what the company says is pneumonia and they're not to blame. You see, they couldn't build the dam with a fast-running, hostile river running through it, so the first step was to divert the water into four enormous tunnels through sheer granite."

Jack consulted his notes again and said, "The tunnels, two on each side of the canyon, had to be blasted through nearly a mile of rock. Each is more than fifty feet in diameter and lined with concrete. They have this enormous machine that backs up into each tunnel in turn and drills the holes for the dynamite, then the men and trucks go in and haul away the debris. These workers, who labor seven days a week with only Christmas Day and the Fourth of July as days off—without pay for those days—are working in really foul air. The atmosphere is dust and carbon monoxide

from the trucks. Sometimes the dust creates so
much electricity that there are explosions."

He paused to look at Mr. Prinney to see what
his reaction was. Had this happened to Mary's
husband? Or wasn't Mary involved at all? Was
Mr. Prinney investigating this on behalf of someone Jack didn't know about?

But Mr. Prinney didn't let on to anything.
"Go on."

"Okey-dokey," Jack said. "Next week the tunnels will go through. The workers will start
dumping the rocks they've removed into the middle of the Colorado River upstream to force the
water into the tunnels. The Six Companies are
about a year ahead of schedule. Next they can
start pouring the concrete for the dam. It'll be as
tall as a sixty-story building."

Mr. Prinney merely nodded. "Aside from the
work schedule, how do the men live?"

Jack riffled through his papers. He knew he
had the information, but couldn't remember
where it was. Finally he found it. "Originally,
there were about two thousand men camping out
on the desert, many with their wives and children
in makeshift tents. Nothing grows there and it's
fiercely hot. There's not even any shade."

He went on, "It's worse in the tunnels. Do you
know, it's sometimes 140 degrees in those tunnels
and the men who are working them don't even
have an adequate fresh water supply? Some who
had vehicles lived in Las Vegas, which I think is

about an hour's drive. But they're building poky little houses at the site now, a town called Boulder City, and have put the single men, and those without wives or children, in dormitories."

He flipped through his notes again. "They're currently hiring many more thousands of men to do the concrete. It's like building blocks. So it can cool before the next layer goes on. Otherwise it wouldn't cool down for nearly twenty years and would probably crack long before that.

"I'd rather starve than do a job like that," he added.

"So would I. I had no idea about the conditions. They sound downright criminal. I wonder that someone with some compassion isn't overseeing it," Mr. Prinney said, sounding very angry.

"There's a huge amount of money involved," Jack said. "It's costing the country over 160 million dollars, and the sooner Mr. Crowe gets it done, the sooner the Six Companies make that money. As soon as it gets working, the government will recover the money by selling the"—he paused to figure out how to pronounce one word—"hydroelectricity, whatever that is, to generate for millions of people in the Southwest."

Chapter 15

After Jack had left, Mr. Prinney called the local operator to set up for a long-distance call. So few people in Voorburg made them, that it took quite a long time for the operator to figure out how to put it through. And this was a difficult situation. He knew the operators often listened in on conversations and warned her that what he had to say was confidential.

He knew the name of the man whose office he needed to call, but had no idea of the city. There had been mention of Las Vegas as the home of some of the workers. There was also a mention of something called Rag Town, which is where the workers lived in tents. Rag Town wouldn't be listed, because he presumed nobody in a tent had a phone.

An hour later, the operator called him back. "I managed to get in touch with the government in Washington. I finally found out that I needed the Department of Commerce. I found a secretary there who gave me the number for Mr. Crowe. Do you still want to be put through?"

"Yes, and I appreciate your good work. Give me the number now, in case I need to call back, if you would."

She did so and said, "I'll let you know when I can put you through."

It was a ten-minute wait.

Mr. Prinney introduced himself to the woman who answered. "I have an important question."

"Mr. Crowe isn't in his office now," the woman said. "I'm his secretary," and she gave her name.

"I don't have to speak directly to him. You may be able to help me."

He explained that he was an attorney who had a client who had received a telegram saying that her husband, who was working on the dam, had died. Further, the name was misspelled. To whom should he speak to arrange to mail a picture of the real person?

The secretary said, "Would you spell the name for me correctly, then spell it the way the telegram said? Speak loudly and slowly so I get it down properly."

He did so and she then said, "I'll look in the files for both names. It may take me a while. Would you mind calling back in two hours? Mr. Crowe doesn't allow anyone but himself to place long-distance calls. They cut into his budget."

"I understand that. And thanks for your help. I'll speak to you later. Thank you very much."

He considered using the two hours to fill in Mrs. Towerton as to what he was doing, but thought better of it. He really didn't know anything positive yet and didn't want to get her hopes up. He felt fairly certain her husband, illiterate and not speaking well because of his injury, had simply been misunderstood when he gave his name. Otherwise, how would they have had his and not some other man's address? Mary Towerton had surely considered this but had said nothing about it. To keep her faint hopes intact, he hadn't mentioned it either.

Jack Summer, unknown to him, was watching his office to see where Mr. Prinney would go next. Jack felt guilty about this bit of sneakiness. He understood why Mr. Prinney wouldn't talk about why he'd asked for the information, but Jack cared a great deal about Mary Towerton.

When he realized he'd waited an hour and a half lurking and the attorney hadn't left his office, he gave up.

When the two hours were almost up, Elgin Prinney once again called the local operator. He asked if she would put him in touch with the number he'd called earlier and let him know when she was through.

The same woman answered. "Oh, Mr. Prinney. You're very prompt. I think I have the name and number of the man you need to contact. He's in charge of the single men's dormitories. I contacted him and explained your problem, but you should get in touch with him yourself so he understands exactly what you need. Here's the information. . . ."

Two expensive long-distance calls, Mr. Prinney thought, and now he had to make a third one. Mr. Prinney wrote the information down.

It took another two hours to get the man. Mr. Prinney explained the whole story again.

"I want to send you a picture of the real Towerton. It was taken before he broke his nose and acquired a serious scar on his lip that apparently made it difficult to understand his speech. If you could show it around to the men who might have known him or recognize him yourself, I could confirm to my client whether she's wife or widow. She'll need to receive a death certificate, if it's the right man. I presume whoever he is has already been buried out there."

"Yes, he's buried. We can disinter him if she wants to bury him at home."

"She can't afford to do that," Mr. Prinney said.

"I see what the problem is with the spelling of his name. Many of the men here are illiterate. We take down their names the best we can. If they're married and don't have a wife along, we get her address. Send along your picture and I'll write and tell you what I can find out."

Mr. Prinney thanked him profusely, hoping it would hurry along the process.

Friday morning while Jack was speaking with Mr. Prinney, Lily was asking Mrs. Tarkington if she'd heard from Miss Langston.

"I haven't yet. I wrote to her at the home ad-

dress I had for her the very day she left, asking
her to let me know how she was getting along.
Most of our teachers are spinsters and if anything
happened to them, I'd have to know how to reach
their families, you see? I imagine Miss Langston
isn't yet well enough to write and report how
she's doing. Perhaps she'll just turn up one day."
She paused, then asked, "Are you or your brother
tired of teaching?"

"No, I'm enjoying it and so is Robert. I'm just
wondering how long we're likely to be doing it. I
fear if and when winter hits us hard, we may not
be able to get up and down the hill in the car. And
if we have a heavy snow, we might have to find
some snowshoes," Lily said with a smile.

Later that same morning, Mrs. Tarkington mo-
tioned Lily to come out of the room. She showed
her an envelope. "My letter to Miss Langston has
come back marked 'Not known at this address.' "

"Oh dear," Lily said.

"I double-checked the record. It was clear and
in her good handwriting. I don't quite know what
to do. Maybe her people moved and she forgot to
tell me. She probably didn't remember I'd ever
asked for her family's address."

Or maybe she didn't go home, Lily thought.

"You mentioned that she has a friend here in
town. I wonder if she would know the proper address?" Lily suggested. "Would you like me to
ask her?"

"That would be very helpful. I certainly don't

want Miss Langston to think we don't care how well she's getting along."

"I've forgotten the name of her friend. I'm not sure you told me."

"It's Miss Amelia Jurgen. And she lives on River Street. A big blue house in the middle of the block between Fifth and Sixth Street. Big garage behind it in the same color. I had to drop Miss Langston off there one day when her car wouldn't start."

"I'll walk over there after lunch and find out if she has the proper address," Lily volunteered.

"I could do it myself, if you prefer," Mrs. Tark-ington said.

"I don't mind a bit. I've never met her and I like getting to know as many people in town as I can."

Lily set off after Robert took over in the after-noon, and found the house easily. It was the biggest on the block. And though there were dormers, the house was wider than it was tall. She knocked at the door and when it opened, she was surprised. This woman looked like a bigger version of Lily's friend and former teacher Miss Addie Johnson. The same fly-away rusty red hair, though younger than Addie.

"I'm Lily Brewster," she said, putting out her hand. "I'm taking part of your friend Miss Langston's teaching duties while she's gone. You must be Miss Jurgen if I'm at the right house."

"Come in, Miss Brewster. I was just making

coffee and rolls as a cold-day snack. Would you like to join me?"

"I'd love to," Lily said.

The house was very old and very big and well cared for, but somewhat oddly arranged. A wall stretched halfway along from front to back from the entry area. She followed Miss Jurgen to the kitchen toward the back of the house. She asked if she could help with the coffee, and Miss Jurgen said, "It's almost ready. And the rolls are in that basket on the counter, if you'd like to take them to the studio in back."

Lily did as she was asked. The studio was the whole width of the back of the house and had high windows at the back end, letting in a lot of light even on this overcast day. Below the windows were corkboards across the long wall. Two worktables filled most of the space and there was a small sitting area at the right of the room with a pair of comfortable chairs and a small table between them.

Miss Jurgen followed along shortly with a tray and cups and little dishes to put the rolls on. "Would you just shove some of that paperwork along the big table closest to us? I'll set the tray down there."

She poured the coffee into very nice china cups that matched the saucers and plates, as did the butter plate and jam pot. Miss Jurgen was an elegant entertainer of drop-in guests. And the rolls, though tiny, were sweet and delicious.

"Mrs. Tarkington told me that you and Miss

Langston had a business. I glanced at some of the designs on that wall and they're lovely."

"We've been pleased with how profitable it is. Especially in the fall, when so many women are doing projects for Christmas. I can't take full credit for the creativity, though. Millicent does the designs and I convert them to patterns. It's easy for embroidery, difficult for needlepoint, which has to be gridded. She can get a bit snippy if I reject one for that reason. She doesn't understand what I do. Just what she does."

"Does your friend Millicent live in the other half of the house? It looks big outside and I noticed the part I came through is much longer than it is wide."

Miss Jurgen said, "When I inherited this house from my great-aunt in 1928, I felt guilty about having so much room. Also greedy," she added with a smile. "I thought first of keeping this whole floor for myself and making the upstairs another apartment. I soon found out that it wasn't practical. When I received a bid for the work, I nearly had a stroke.

"The builder then suggested the obvious," she went on. "That when someone lives above you, you hear every step they take. Every flush of the toilet. Every door closing or opening. I really didn't want to know *that* much about a renter.

"He suggested that I divide the downstairs and he'd put a lot of air space and horsehair in the barrier to solve the problem, as well as putting one of the 'front' doors on the side. I'd always lived in far less space than I have, and it cost so much less that I did it his way."

"That all sounds very sensible," Lily said.

"I have to admit, too, that Millicent Langston isn't really a friend. She's an employee. We seldom even see each other. She leaves the designs on her table. I convert them on mine. I also handle the selling."

She smiled. "I suppose you already know that she's a great teacher, but doesn't have the gift of getting along well with adults. She does live in the other part of the house. She has her own entrance and"—Miss Jurgen gestured to the other end of the room—"she has her own door to the studio. We each have our privacy and both like it that way. We hardly ever even see each other."

"So you probably won't be able to answer the question I came to ask you," Lily said. "Mrs. Tarkington sent a letter to her asking how she was doing and when she hoped to return. It came back undeliverable at the address she'd given as her family home. Do you happen to have a newer address?"

"I've never had any other address for her. I didn't even know she had a family. She never talks about one. I guess I always assumed she was orphaned young. I didn't really want to be chummy with her. When she said she was going home for this surgery, it surprised me. As I say, she's not very sociable."

"I wonder—well, if she is coming back?"

"I suppose so. She stands to lose her teaching

job and this job if she doesn't. The school won't
have trouble replacing her. As for her job here,
I've been doing this work long enough, I could
certainly do it all myself by now and not have to
pay anyone part of the profits. It was always hard
to convert her artwork to grids. If I made more
money, I could probably get my car fixed. It
hasn't worked for two months and I could find
myself needing to go somewhere I can't walk."

They chatted a little bit longer about how the
work was done, and Miss Jurgen showed some of
her current projects after they finished the coffee
and rolls.

"I must be getting back home. I've taken up far
too much of your valuable time," Lily said. "I've
enjoyed our visit. I'm glad to have met you and
admire your skills. And your entertaining."

"I've enjoyed it, too. You must come back. I seldom have company, as much as I'd like to."

On the way to the front door, Miss Jurgen
showed Lily a few of the pieces she'd actually
done herself. They were on pillows and pillow-
cases and were exquisitely produced.

"Could you consider teaching me the basics?"
Lily asked. "I could never do this as well as you
do, but I'd like to learn."

"I'd love to. After the holidays is my slow time
of year. We could plan a regular time and day.
And I can try out some new recipes for you."

Lily went away smiling. She liked this woman
and needed a good friend here in Voorburg.

Chapter 16

On the same day Lily met Miss Jurgen, Chief Walker decided it was time to visit the Institute. He drove up the river road early in the morning and crossed the bridge over the Hudson, wondering all the while if everyone had already cleared out. When he found the place, he saw that it was housed in one of the old mansions but was set back from a river view.

What had served as the home base of the Institute of Divine Intervention was a big sprawling house and probably dated from the late part of the previous century. He parked the police car in the circular drive and tried the front door, which was open. The large, neglected entry hall was eerily silent except for the tap of a distant typewriter being used somewhere upstairs. He glanced around and decided he'd explore a bit before he hunted down the typist.

A large room, probably a former parlor, to the left, had been tarted up to serve as Pottinger's office. The once-beautiful tapestry wallpaper had been covered with pictures of Brother Goodheart preaching, or shaking hands with celebrities who supported him, or showing off the downtrodden he had claimed to help out. The desk was huge and had obviously been chosen for size rather than style or taste.

He took a look in the drawers, but they were empty except for a few crumbs of paper, a couple of pens, and some loose staples. Chief Leland Colling and his staff had done a good job. There was a small anteroom attached that was apparently where Edward Price had worked. It was empty of everything but the furniture.

He crossed the hall into what had once been a grand banquet hall. It had retained most of its former glory, except that it was unkempt. The elaborate glass chandelier drops were grimy, the enormous table dusty, and stacks of paperwork and random office files were piled on it.

He glanced through several of the piles. They all seemed to be typed transcripts and carbon copies of Pottinger's speeches. A collection of radios had been heaped in the far corner of the room. Apparently a lot of cleaning out was being done. He wondered what would happen to these things.

He then went in search of the source of the typing sounds. At the top of the steps there was an office with an open door. A tall, plain, middle-aged woman in trousers, a checkered shirt, and an old blue sweater looked up at him from the typewriter.

"May I help you?" she asked.

"I'm Chief of Police Howard Walker from Voorburg."

"The gentleman handling the murder, I assume," she said calmly. "Sit down if you can find a chair." Her office seemed to be the paperwork center. "I'm about the only one left here, and I'm trying to clear things out." She stood up, came around the desk, and shook his hand. "Mrs. Taylor at your service. Let me move some of this so you can be comfortable."

She wasn't the least alarmed by his visit. "So what do you need from me?" she said pleasantly, resuming her place behind the desk.

"Tell me a bit about yourself, if you would. Have you worked here long?"

"Almost since the beginning, when Pottinger bought this pile," she said with a smile. "About seven years ago."

"And what is your job?"

"Right now or when I started?"

"Both."

"I was originally the receptionist. Had a desk in the entry hall and told visitors where to find whomever they were looking for. Pottinger decided I wasn't attractive enough for that," she said wryly. "But I was a good worker and he set me up here to handle the mail that came in."

"Did you admire the man in charge?"

"Pottinger? Admire Pottinger?" She almost laughed. "Not at all. He was a bigot, but I'd mar-

ried late to an older man who died when my
daughter was twelve, and I needed a job to support us. It could have been worse. I received a
good salary, of which I've saved quite a lot. I
wasn't pretty enough for him to bother with."

"And why are you staying on?"

"I'm still on salary, helping the attorney close
down the place. And Pottinger left me an annuity.
When I finish, I'll be all right financially. My
daughter's just married a man with a good job.
One of the few men left who has one."

"What does closing down the Institute involve?"

"Quite a number of things. I'm working with
the attorney to hunt down Pottinger's son, for
one thing."

It hadn't occurred to Walker that Jackson Kinsey was probably Pottinger's executor and would
be paid generously to administer the estate. Another reason he couldn't afford to disappear.

"Pottinger has a family?"

"Only the son, as far as I know. He was married
in the early days in Nebraska and left his wife
and boy behind. She divorced him and later died,
I understand."

"How old is this son?"

"Nineteen, almost twenty."

"Were they on good terms?"

"Decidedly not. It seemed from the boy's letters that Pottinger was always trying to drag
him up here, but the boy—his name is Charles,
Jr.—wanted nothing to do with him. The last I

knew of him, he was living in Wheeling, West Virginia."

"How did you know that?"

"They corresponded and I handle the mail. I open all of it and send it along to whomever it needs to go to. I never saw, of course, Pottinger's letters to him, just the son's responses. Which were pretty heated and critical."

"How long ago was this? When he was in West Virginia?"

She thought for a moment. "I'd guess about a year ago."

Yet another elusive suspect, Howard thought, who stood to inherit a fortune and had a good motive.

"I'm also trying to figure out what to do with the orphans," Mrs. Taylor went on. "That's especially hard to do. I've managed to find people to adopt two of them, but there are still six of them here, with one teacher. You wouldn't like to take one, would you?"

Walker shook his head. "I'm single. I couldn't take care of a child. But I'll ask around Voorburg. Maybe Mrs. White, our local do-gooder, could help out."

"Would you like me to show you the rest of the place?"

"I certainly would, if you have the time."

She showed him the rest of the second floor first. Most of the bedrooms on the north wing had been converted to offices. The offices of both

Jackson Kinsey, the sleazy attorney, and Big Jimmy Rennie, the treasurer, were opulent. Nobby Hazard's was bleak and still stank of his hair oil.

The south wing consisted of only two bedrooms. One was gigantic and flamboyant, with a large fireplace, a huge bed with a canopy of red velvet, a well-stocked bar with silver decanters and crystal glasses, and a vast bathroom with a deep tub complete with gold fittings. Pottinger didn't stint on his luxuries. It looked like a high-class whorehouse.

Edward Price had a modest bedroom next to Pottinger's disgusting one. Price's room was neat and efficient and had nothing personal except a picture of a young woman who was probably a girlfriend or maybe the sister he was staying with. A few of his clothes that he hadn't yet taken away were hanging in the closet.

The rest of the rooms were for the daily drudges—the men and women who sent out the fliers announcing Pottinger's speeches. These offices were empty and abandoned.

This reminded Walker of the address book. When the tour was done, he'd have to have a talk with Mrs. Taylor about the women whose names had been crossed out in it.

Next Mrs. Taylor showed him around the outbuildings. The garage contained two very expensive touring cars. "I don't suppose you know anyone who'd take these off our hands?"

"I'm afraid not. I don't know anybody with that kind of money."

"They'll go cheap," she said with a smile. "Practically anybody who can afford to buy the gas to run them could buy them for a pittance."

He smiled back at her. "I'll see if our Mrs. White knows anybody. She might want to contribute one of them to our minister. He's driving an ancient wreck she claims is below his dignity."

The building next to the garage was a big shed, nearly empty. It contained only an old lawn mower, a couple of loppers, clippers, some incidental hardware, and a toolbox. He'd noticed on his approach to the Institute that the grounds had no gardens whatsoever. Just paths and grass. One room of the shed contained a bed, a hot plate, an empty wardrobe, and a primitive bathroom set up in the corner.

"This obviously belonged to the groundskeeper," Mrs. Taylor said. "He's gone now. If we can't unload this place until spring comes, we'll have to find someone else to cut the grass."

She then led him to a house that looked like a converted barn behind the two structures. It was a moderately sized but shabby house.

Mrs. Taylor said, "This is where the orphans live. Come meet them."

The remaining children appeared to Walker to range in age from five to eleven or twelve years old. They were adequately well dressed and apparently healthy. There was no sign of the work they had previously done making the collection baskets except some little nicks and scars on their hands. It made him hate Pottinger even more than before.

There was a side room with little cots that broke Walker's heart. The room was barren. The sheets and blankets were coarse and ugly. The beds themselves were obviously too small for some of the larger, older children.

The big middle workroom was now a classroom where an elderly lady was teaching them to read.

Mrs. Taylor told Walker, "This is Miss Perkins, who's staying on for a while. Miss Perkins, this is Chief of Police Walker from Voorburg. He's in charge of"—she lowered her voice so the children couldn't hear—"the murder investigation."

"I'm pleased to meet you," Miss Perkins said in a sweet and surprisingly young-sounding voice. She turned to Mrs. Taylor and said plaintively, "I wish we could get Miss Waywright back. She was much better than I am at this."

She went back to the youngest children, two pretty little blond girls who were learning the alphabet. The other children just stared at him with blank looks.

Walker decided then and there that he'd have to bring Mrs. White up here and tempt her to do "good works." Nobody was bossier or better at it.

Chapter 17

Friday afternoon, Mr. Prinney went to see Mary Towerton to tell her what he was doing. She immediately suggested, in a whisper, that they go outside to talk. She threw a warm shawl over herself and baby Emily. "My son is almost four years old and understands a lot of what he hears. I don't think the baby does. I'll let him play on the swing while we talk."

The little boy had followed them out on the porch, struggling into his coat. Mary said, "Joey, say 'How do you do?' to Mr. Prinney."

Joey put his little hand out to shake Mr. Prinney's and did as he'd been told.

"You may go play on the swing Daddy made for you," she said. As he whooped and ran to the swing, Mary, with the baby in her arms, and Mr. Prinney sat down in two badly frayed wicker chairs. He was glad she didn't apologize for their condition.

"I need to explain a little background," Mr. Prinney said. He decided not to go into the whole

history of the dam and the company associations
Jack had told him about, and started with the tunnels. "The companies involved couldn't start
building the dam with the river flowing through
the deep chasm."

"I understand," she said.

"So they had to divert the water first. They
built two enormous tunnels on each side through
solid rock." He spared her a description of the terrible heat, the carbon monoxide poisoning, the
lack of fresh water, the grueling work schedule,
and the criminal disregard for safety. He said
only, "This work has caused a lot of accidents.
Falling rocks, injuries, illnesses, and deaths."

"Are you telling me I'm a widow?" She
mouthed the last word over Emily's head.

"No. I'm just giving you the picture of the
work. Many of the men who do the labor have
their families along, and they're either living in
tents on the site or small houses that are being
built for them. They also have dormitories for single men and men without families with them.
Your husband probably lived in one of these. I've
been in touch with the man who manages them—
he handles the food, the room assignments, disputes, and such. I've just sent a copy of your
wedding picture, explaining that it was taken before his accident with the tractor, and he says he'll
show it to the men who might have known him
as Rick Taughton instead of Richard Towerton."

"Do you think he'll really do that?"

"We can only hope so."

"Do you have any idea how long this will take?" she asked.

Prinney admired her calm and sensible questions. This couldn't be easy for her, but she wasn't a sniveler.

"It could be within two weeks. However, he's probably a busy man, so I think it will take a little more time than that. It's a long way to send the letter and picture and a long way back for the reply."

"I realize that. What if this person doesn't get around to it at all?"

"I think he will," Mr. Prinney said. "I explained the situation to him in detail on the telephone and also in the letter I sent with the picture. Oh, I have the original to give back to you," he said, taking it from his briefcase along with a typed copy of the letter. "I'll contact you immediately when I hear back."

When the adults rose carefully from the chairs, Joey ran back, his face nicely pink from his exertions. Mary said, "Joey, please tell Mr. Prinney how nice it was to meet him."

He parroted his mother shyly and ran inside.

Mary stood on the porch, waving as Mr. Prinney chugged off in his Ford. Then she walked slowly into the house. She put Emily in the crib that Richard had made for Joey, and read the copy of Mr. Prinney's letter. It was formal, of course, but it wrung her heart and she hoped it would also touch the man at the work site.

She looked again at the wedding picture.

"Mommy, you sad?" Joey asked.

"No. Look at this picture." She sat down in a chair and pulled him up on her lap. "Who's this?" she said, pointing at herself in the picture.

He giggled. "You, Mommy!"

"And who is the other person."

"Daddy?"

"Yes, that's your daddy."

But she knew from the question in his voice that he didn't remember him. She'd showed him the picture and taught him that was his daddy, but she didn't think he really knew what it meant. Daddy to him was a person who'd made the swing and the crib. Not somebody he'd really known, except maybe in his dreams.

That night Mary had to face up to herself for real. Which answer did she really want? In a way, she'd been a widow for more than two years already. She was starting not to mind too much. No, that wasn't quite the truth. She'd started not minding a long time ago.

She'd learned quite a lot about taking care of herself and her children, one of whom Richard probably didn't even know existed.

She'd learned to take care of the bad-tempered old mule and knew how to hitch him up to the wagon. She'd been forced to learn to use tools and fix things around the house when something went wrong. She would take the children with her, Emily in the old pram, Joey on foot, into the woods and find firewood for the stove. She'd come home pushing the pram and dragging Joey's little wagon behind with the wood in it.

She'd written to tell her husband about dear little Emily, but of course she'd addressed the letter to Richard Towerton at Boulder Dam, Arizona. If they had no record of his real name, it would probably have been thrown away.

She wrote again last summer when her grandfather died and was buried in Maryland. She'd composed it on her way back from taking Grandfather in the buckboard to the Bonus Army March. Richard probably hadn't received that letter either.

If he had, surely he'd have somebody read it to him and ask them to write back for him. He'd done that once before when he went up to Sarasota Springs to bury his father and stayed on for a couple of winter weeks to sell the family farm.

Joey became fidgety and she let him go play with his blocks by the stove. The blocks were another thing she'd improved. When Joey had gotten a little splinter from one of them, she'd sanded them and painted them bright colors.

She sat staring at the wedding picture. She looked happy and pretty on that day. But not in love. She admired how hard Richard worked and how kind he was to her impossible grandfather. She liked Richard. And she wanted babies. It seemed then to be a good enough reason to marry before she grew older and her grandfather scared off all her beaus. She'd been terrified that she might become a childless spinster.

She found herself thinking back to the day she buried her grandfather. Jack Summer had collected enough money from strangers who were also fleeing the devastation of the camp on the Anacostia Flats to buy a very cheap coffin and get the tough, crabby old man into the ground.

But she always tried to put Jack Summer at the back of her mind. When she'd returned and found out that he'd been staying at her house, waiting for her return while he wrote up his articles about the Bonus March, she'd been downright rude to him. She'd never stopped regretting that she'd spoken out without thinking. She should have been far more tactful and not said what she did.

If, as she suspected strongly, she *was* a widow . . .

She woke the next morning, angry with herself for having a slightly unseemly dream about Jack Summer.

Chief Walker didn't need to haul Mrs. Edith White up to the Institute. When she heard about the orphans and the cars, she hotfooted it up to meet Mrs. Taylor the very next day. Dealing first with the automobiles, she purchased the big white-with-red-trim 1931 Peerless for the minister, at the bargain price of five hundred dollars.

"How nice it will be for him to be able to take a

lot of the children out in the country," Mrs. White said.

Mrs. Taylor smiled. She'd never seen a "real" minister who would be caught dead in such a vehicle. Neither had she ever looked a gift horse in the mouth. She did warn Mrs. White that the Peerless automobile plant was no longer in business and it would be hard to make repairs on it.

Mrs. White replied confidently that automobiles were all alike inside, so it wouldn't make any difference. Mrs. Taylor thought she'd done her best and didn't disabuse Mrs. White of this concept.

Mrs. Taylor was certain that the minister himself hadn't been consulted and that the last thing he would want was to haul a bunch of children anywhere in the garish big automobile.

Next Mrs. White questioned the children. Could they read? Could they prove it? Were they healthy and strong? She looked them over so closely that even their ears were examined to make sure they were both clean and working.

Miss Perkins, their only teacher now, pointed out that the two youngest girls, pretty little things with blond curls, were sisters.

"I'll take them myself," Mrs. White said, deciding on the spot. "I think two of the bigger boys could go with farmers who don't have sons to help with their crops. I'll get back to you about this and have my attorney draw up the papers."

After packing up their few pitiful belongings,

she took the two little girls home and gave them good baths. Then she carted them off to Poughkeepsie to buy several sets of matching frocks.

Walker himself also went back to the Institute to talk to Miss Taylor again after calling ahead to see if she was working there on a Saturday. She said she'd be there until two o'clock. He'd been so distressed the last time he was there and saw the orphans in their pitiful state that he'd forgotten to ask her about Pottinger's address book.

This time he brought the book along. He asked her about the women's names that had been crossed out. Not all had home addresses, but some did.

Mrs. Taylor went over the list carefully. "I suppose most of the local women are still nearby." She pointed out Tabitha Riley, Susanna Cooper, and Joan Wilton. "You can probably find them home with their families. But some don't even have home addresses listed. Here is Mildred Waywright, for example. She's the teacher Miss Perkins mentioned who taught the orphans. She was a good teacher, but objected to the children making baskets without getting time for being educated. I remember her because she took her complaint directly to Pottinger and was gone the next day. Nobody was allowed to tell him off."

She ran her finger back up the list. "Here's another who complained to Pottinger and told everyone he'd made an indecent proposal to one of her friends. She read the riot act to him in a scalding letter. Kathryn Staley. He's crossed out her home address too thoroughly to read it. I think she was from somewhere up north. Boston, I think. I'm sorry I can't help with most of them.

"It's a shame they were dismissed," she went on. "They were all nice, decent young women who believed in Brother Goodheart and wanted to further his cause. Until they learned who and what he really was."

She glanced at her watch, then at the piles of paperwork on her desk, and added, "Good luck with your search. And thanks so much for putting me in touch with Mrs. White. She really is a force of nature, isn't she?"

Chapter 18

Howard's next stop was to pick up Lily at Grace and Favor while Robert, with the help of the Harbinger boys, put the guest suite back to the way it had been before Pottinger and his gang had come.

"Howard, who are you looking for?" Robert asked.

"I have a question for Lily."

"She walked to town to take some library books back. I'm supposed to pick her up in a half an hour."

"I'll fetch her myself and bring her back later," Howard said.

She was just coming out of the library with a heavy parcel of books when he found her.

"Want a lift? Robert told me where you were."

"You bet!" she said, fearing she sounded too much like Robert. "Is your car warm?"

At his nod, she piled in and said, "You aren't hauling me off to the asylum, are you?"

"Next best thing. I need your help. I want to interview several of the women whose names are marked off in this address book," he said, handing it to her to glance through. "The questions will be rather 'personal,' if you know what I mean."

"Oh?" Lily said warily.

"About Pottinger/Goodheart. His relationships, or would-be relationships, with them. Young women aren't likely to talk frankly to a cop. I thought I might take you to see them, then I'll fade into the background. They would feel more secure talking to another woman."

"What good will this do you to find out?"

"I'm not quite sure. But they're all suspects of a sort. 'A woman scorned' and all that can be dangerous, if not downright unhinged."

Lily looked startled. "You think one of these women is such an idiot that she's going to break down and confess to a perfect stranger, man *or* woman?"

"Odder things have happened," Howard said weakly. He was sorry he'd started this conversation. "You could just say you had recent contact with Brother Goodheart and are still deeply upset. You don't have to be specific. Someone told you they knew him, too, and see if they take the bait."

Lily sighed. She would very much like to know who had murdered someone in the sanctity of her own home. And it gave her the willies to think that that person was still free to roam around and possibly take another life.

Besides this, Chief Walker had never truly asked her to help him before, though she and Robert had offered him information that led to catching criminals. The one-upmanship this would afford her in relation to Robert pleased her.

"All right. Let's try out one of the ladies and see what happens. I'll probably be thrown out of their house in disgrace. How far away do these people live?"

"Not more than a half hour's drive. One way."

"May I drop my books off at home first?"

Lily delivered her message to Robert as intriguingly as she could manage. He was helping the Harbinger boys get the big table down the stairs. Lily whispered, "Howard Walker's asked me to help him out with something. I might not get back for a little while."

"What? What?"

She just smiled as she slipped away down the hall. She loved it that he was so curious. Score one for her.

Following the order in Pottinger's address book, the first address they went to was that of Tabitha Riley. It was the closest to Voorburg, only about a third of the way up Route 9 to Poughkeepsie. It was a shabby little house in a shabby neighborhood. The step to the front door was crooked and disintegrating. What had once been a garden was a patch of weeds, and paint was peeling. But oddly, the older woman who came to the door was elegantly dressed in an old-fashioned, though stylish, silk frock. She wore it with a triple strand of real pearls that should have weighed her down.

Walker told her whom they were looking for.

"The Rileys moved out two years ago. June Riley was my maid and her husband wanted to go to California to get work. Here I am, living in my maid's house while mine is due to be auctioned for taxes."

This broke Lily's heart. Walker had to harden his. "Did you know their daughter Tabitha?" he asked her.

"Very slightly. When she was around fourteen, she used to help out when I gave parties. She was vegetable peeler. Not a very nice girl, I'm afraid. Pretty and obedient. But dumb as a rabbit."

"Have you heard from the Rileys since they left?"

"No. I'm not likely to either. Sorry I can't help you. Has Tabitha done something bad?"

"No. We just needed some information from her about the Institute of Divine Intervention."

"Did she end up working for that awful man?" the woman said with a look of disgust. "I guess that shouldn't surprise me."

As they turned to leave, Lily said quietly, "I hope things get better for you."

The woman's eyes reddened and she croaked, "Thank you."

On the way to the next address, Howard tried

to cheer Lily up by saying, "Your hair's looking better."

"I got that awful permanent in order to pry information out of the hairdresser for your use. I'm glad you noticed." Lily's light, short "do" had been fried by an electric permanent months ago, and Mrs. Prinney's recommended treatment of soaking her hair in mayonnaise once a week had helped.

Next on the list was Joan Wilton. She lived quite near the Riley house, also in a bad neighborhood. She herself came to the door. "My, my, aren't you a handsome man?" she gushed, ogling Walker. "What's up, big guy?"

She was a skinny girl with a thin, fawnlike face and dirty fingernails. Her hair could have profited from being washed. The clothes she was wearing were skimpy and needed cleaning and ironing badly.

He showed her his badge. She giggled. "Come on in, you and your girlfriend," she said and whirled around in order to show a lot of a shapely leg when her short skirt couldn't catch up with her quick move.

Lily thought it must have taken a lot of practice in front of a mirror to do that so well.

Joan Wilton headed for the sagging brown sofa and cleared a selection of beat-up books from its cushions by dumping them onto the floor. Their covers featured salacious pictures. She brushed some cracker crumbs off as well and sat down in the middle.

"Sit yourself down next to me," she said with a wink at Walker. "You, miss, can sit on the straight chair."

The straight chair must have been used as a table for sugary drinks, and Lily felt her skirt sticking to it.

"So whaddya want, big guy?" Joan said.

Walker had perched on the arm of the sofa instead of accepting her invitation, and it was so cheap it wobbled. He took a notebook out of his suit pocket and said, "I understand that you once worked at the Institute of Divine Intervention."

"Boy, did I ever," Joan said with a laugh. "That old goat who preached was always pawing me when he thought no one was looking. What a creep. But a girl's gotta eat, doesn't she?"

"Why did you leave the job?"

"For one thing, they paid peanuts. I'd been getting better money working at Myer's Clam Tavern." She put her hand to her mouth as if she'd accidentally said something delightfully naughty. "Tips, I mean."

Sure you do, Lily thought. Robert had told her about the "working girls" who lived on the third floor.

"Then, when the old creep of a preacher took me up to his room and wanted—well, you know what," she said with another giggle, "I said to him I didn't come free and I'd only charge him a fifty-cent-an-hour raise in my salary as long as I stayed at the place. Boy oh boy, you should have seen him! Here he is all dolled up in a fancy striped satin robe with his you-know-what poking out the front. Kinda puny, really. He turned all high and mighty, stomping around the room yelling about Whores of Babylon and eternal damnation and all that stuff."

She suddenly looked up at Walker with a seductive smile. A smile that would have been improved enormously by seeing a dentist once in a while, Lily thought.

"While he was busy with his arms up in the air yelling at God through the ceiling, I just picked up a few of those little pretty ornaments on the bedside table and nipped right out. Got a whole twelve dollars when I pawned them."

Lily peeled her skirt off the chair and headed for the door. She waited outside until Howard joined her seconds later.

"I think," he said, his face quite red, "she's not a suspect. After all, she made twelve dollars."

"I don't want to go on with this," Lily said. "I've never met a girl like that and don't want to run into any more of them."

"Just one more, please," Howard pleaded. "I can leave you on the doorstep if the next one is like this one."

"Who's going to protect *you*?"

He took her arm abruptly and walked her back

to the police car. "I was only offended on your behalf," he snapped.

Once they were in the car, he turned to her and
said, calmly, "Look, Lily, we only have two more
who might still be living at the addresses in Pottinger's book. Would you stick with me for at
least one more?"

"Is that an apology?"

"Yes," he admitted.

The third former secretary on the list lived just
south of Voorburg. It was getting late. The old
trees made it dark and hard to find the house on
the winding street. When they located it, it was
fairly respectable. They were met by a very plain
young woman with her hair in braids around her
head framing her wide, bland face. "Yes?" she
said as if they were trying to sell her something.

"Are you Susanna Cooper?"

"No. But she lives here, too. Is it she you want
to see?"

"Yes, if it's convenient," Walker said politely.

"What do you want of her?" Lily noticed the
young woman was holding a Bible in her hand
with her forefinger holding the page she'd apparently been reading.

"Just to ask a few questions," Walker said,
showing her his badge.

Her face went white. "What do you want of
poor Susanna? Hasn't she put up with enough already?"

"I'd like to ask her myself," Walker said firmly, walking inside.

It was a very small, tidy house, with rag rugs on the floor, a small wood fire in the grate, and pictures of Jesus on nearly every wall of the front room.

The girl with the braids went through a door and closed it behind her. Lily and Walker sat down on padded chairs with crocheted afghans either protecting them or covering up the flaws. They could hear whispering behind the door.

In a few minutes, the young woman with the braids came back leading a lovely girl. A valentine face, very pale, with a mass of glossy black, curly hair surrounding it. She looked like a porcelain figurine and appeared to be just as fragile.

"I'm Susanna," she said. The two friends sat down on two wooden chairs across from Lily and Walker. The one with the braid hitched her chair closer to the other girl.

Walker introduced himself and said he was there to ask her about Brother Goodheart.

Susanna's pale blue eyes filled with tears. "I really don't want to talk about him."

"I'm afraid you must," Walker said very gently.

Chapter 19

It's all *my* fault!" the girl with the braids exclaimed in a loud, abrasive voice.

"Before you explain that, what is your name?" Walker asked.

"I'm Kathryn Staley."

Walker exchanged glances with Lily. That was the last name on their list. But her address had been crossed through. Mrs. Taylor at the Institute had said she'd resigned by letter, complaining of abuse of a friend. They'd bagged two for one.

"What is your fault and why, Miss Staley?"

"It's not," Susanna said. "I've told you so a million times, Kathryn."

"I went to work for the Institute," Kathryn went on, ignoring her friend's warning. "I honestly thought Brother Goodheart was the greatest man in the world. So powerful, so generous, such a wonderful speaker for the rights of downtrodden Americans and good Christians. I liked his idea of a Hitler or Mussolini figure for our country. Those are the sort of men who won't waffle around when trouble comes. And what choice did we have here? A man who did nothing running against a cripple! So I suggested that Susanna take a job at the Institute as well. Susanna's awfully smart, knows her English, types really well, and was out of work."

Lily thought, what with the blond braids, broad, pale, Aryan face, as well as her attitude, she'd make a perfect Brunhilde for Hitler.

"So you were approved for the job?" Walker made a point of talking to Susanna and shifted in his chair so that he was directly facing her.

"Yes, I was. And I enjoyed it—for a while. Brother Goodheart complimented me a lot on my work. Then"—she paused and took a deep breath, "he invited me up to his room. His bedroom, I mean. Not his office. I didn't want to go. He said he had a little gold cross he wanted to give me since I was such a good Christian girl. I was afraid not to. I really needed the job."

She put her hands over her face for a moment. "It was so horrible. At first I didn't know what was going on. He left me looking at the cross and went into another room and came out wearing a silk robe. He—well, he exposed his privates to me." She blushed bright pink. "I tried to run for the door, but he snatched me by the elbow and threw me on the bed and started tearing at my clothes and . . ."

"Go ahead and say it, Susanna," Kathryn said.

Susanna whispered, "He raped me. I kept trying to fight him off and I was crying something horrible and he started hitting me in the face." She pulled back one side of her curly dark hair that cupped around her temple and showed them a still somewhat red scar.

"I finally escaped and ran out of the room, down the stairs, and outside. I ran toward home, here, until I could hardly breathe. I had to lie down in the woods for a while before I could go on."

She leaned over, propped her elbows on her knees, covered her eyes again, and sobbed.

Kathryn took over the conversation again. "Several people saw her run out and I heard them talking about Susanna running down the stairs and outside all bloody with her clothes torn. I raced to try to find out what happened and where she'd gone. But I couldn't find her. I drove straight home. She wasn't there." She held her hands as though she were praying.

"I drove back toward the Institute, looking along the side of the road for her. By the time it was dark, I went home and here she was. I took her to the hospital in Poughkeepsie."

"Did she tell them who did this to her?" Walker asked.

"Yes, I did," Susanna said, lowering her hands. "And they didn't believe me. The doctor became really mad at me for saying bad things about a fine Christian example of a man, and said I was covering for a boyfriend. I've never in my life *had* a boyfriend."

"I backed her up on what she'd said," Kathryn butted in again. "And the next day I sent in my resignation directly to Brother Goodheart, telling him just what I thought of him."

Walker suddenly felt he'd heard enough from Susanna's friend. "Miss Staley, I don't think you quite realize this isn't about you. It's about Miss Cooper."

"Well! I like that!" she said sarcastically, her placid, fat white face growing red and blotchy. "I really do blame myself for not seeing through him. And now I hear he's dead and I'm glad."

"I'm *not* glad," Walker said. "I wish I had him alive to take him to trial and put him away in the nastiest prison in the country to live out a long, miserable life."

He turned again to Susanna. "May I tell this story—without your name, of course—to a reporter I know?"

"Oh, please don't. I don't want anyone else to know. And I never want to talk about this again. It's too upsetting. If you hadn't been from the police, I wouldn't ever have told anyone but Kathryn."

"I promise he wouldn't use your name," Walker pleaded.

"He'd want to hear it directly from me, then know where I live. We already considered moving away because Brother Goodheart knew our address. If we had to leave this sweet little house we love, I simply couldn't bear it."

Walker gave up. "If you feel so strongly, I'll keep this as quiet as I can," he said. "But Brother Goodheart's disciples really should know what kind of brute he was. Think about it, Miss Cooper. You don't need to go anywhere. I'll probably be back in touch with you."

Walker shook hands with Susanna, thanked her for telling him, and apologized for putting her through the ordeal. He said nothing to Kathryn. Without even appearing to notice she was in the room, he gestured to Lily that they were leaving. She followed him.

"I wish I could dig that bastard up and put him on display," he said bitterly as he started the car.

"Put Brunhilde next to him," Lily said.

He stared at her for a long moment, then broke out laughing when he realized she was referring to Miss Staley. When he'd wiped his eyes and settled down, he said, "At least we have a real suspect."

"Not Susanna?"

"No. Brunhilde. She's so determined to take the blame. She really wants to take the credit. I think she's in love with Susanna. It could have been a crime of passion and revenge." He hoped Lily wouldn't be shocked that he thought this.

Lily wasn't offended. She'd gone to pricey girls' schools in the twenties when some of the girls thought it was brazen and interesting to consider themselves lesbians.

"Good motive," Lily said. "Not practical

though. How would Brunhilde have known where he was? And why did she wait so long? That scar on Susanna isn't all that recent."

Howard thought for a few minutes. "Maybe Miss Staley was keeping an eye on him. Parking her car near the Institute and watching where he went. But he usually only left where there'd be crowds around to tear her apart if she attacked him. If she saw him going to Grace and Favor . . ."

"She wouldn't have known where to find him in that mansion," Lily said. "There are still rooms even I haven't been in. And how would she have known his door wasn't locked?" In fact, Lily thought, this applied to all of the secretaries and teachers he'd spoken to.

"Nobody knew that except you and the other residents and guests," Walker said. "But there is such a thing as a lock pick, you know. She could have shinnied up trees and looked in windows with lights to find out which room he was in. She looks like the kind of sturdy woman who would be well able to hoist herself up a tree with no trouble."

"You're fishing, Howard. Just because we both feel sorry for Susanna and despise Kathryn Staley." She said this sympathetically. She'd have liked to agree with him, but couldn't.

"Maybe you're right," he admitted.

"I think it had to be someone who knew Grace and Favor," Lily said. "And it certainly wasn't any of us who live there. So it has to be someone he brought from the Institute.

"The guests all knew the room wasn't locked," she went on. "If the rape was common knowledge at the Institute and Nobby Hazard found out, couldn't he have done it? He's as nuts as Pottinger was and was devoted to him. Just think how betrayed he would have felt if he'd known, and then discovered that Pottinger was also stealing the money. More than enough motive for Nobby to knock his former idol off his pedestal."

"He's still my best guess, too," Howard said. "He may be nuts but that doesn't mean he's either stupid or deaf."

Chapter 20

Howard Walker returned Lily home well in time for dinner and went back to his office at the boardinghouse. The phone was ringing.

"Chief Walker! This is Mrs. Towerton," she said breathlessly. "My son is missing. Please get help and come out with as many people as you can to search for him. I don't have a telephone, so I'm calling from my neighbor's house. I'm on my way home right this minute."

She hung up on a sob.

Walker immediately rousted Ralph and told him to call Mr. Prinney as well, as he dashed for the police car.

When he arrived at Mary Towerton's house with the siren going, she was sitting on the front porch holding her son in one arm. Baby Emily was on her shoulder. Both Mary and the little boy were crying.

"I'm sorry, Chief Walker. He was sitting here when I came home. This note was pinned to his jacket."

Walker took the note by the corner. It was on coarse, reused brown wrapping paper that had stains and creases as if it had been found in someone's trash. It said, in badly printed pencil lettering, *The next time you tatle on me to the lawer he won't be brot back.*

"What does this mean to you?" Walker asked.

Mary blew her nose and sent Joey inside to get his hands washed for dinner. "I have no idea. He says a lady took him for a car ride."

"Can he describe her?"

Ralph pulled up on a motorcycle with his cousin Jack Summer in the sidecar as Walker was asking this question.

"He's not even four years old yet," Mary replied. "He just said she was a lady in a big car who took him for a ride. Of course, any automobile would seem big to him. I don't think he's ever been in one before."

"How do you want us to start the search?" Ralph asked, running to the front porch. "It's almost dark. I brought all the flashlights I could find and a couple of kerosene lamps."

Walker was amazed that Ralph had even thought of these practicalities. He'd never done so before.

"The boy is back," Chief Walker said. "No need for a search."

"Is Joey all right?" Jack asked Mary.

"He seems to be. When he saw me coming, he ran to me as if nothing very interesting had happened. He'd been playing on the swing before he disappeared. I went in the house, just for a few seconds to make sure the stew wasn't burning, and when I came back out to call him in, there was no sign of him."

She put her hand to her heart and hiccuped. "I'll never let him out of my sight again, even for that long. I'm sorry I dragged all of you out here for nothing."

"It isn't nothing," Walker said. "You and your child have been threatened. Even though your son was brought home, he was kidnapped for a short time. That's illegal and I intend to find out who did it if I can. Ralph, did you think of bringing an evidence envelope or two along?"

"Sure did, Chief," Ralph said smugly, going back to the motorcycle to fetch one.

Walker put the note that had been pinned to Joey's jacket into the envelope. "We'll get this fingerprinted as soon as we can, Mrs. Towerton. Ralph and Jack, you boys can go back to what you were doing now. Thanks for being so prompt. And efficient," he added to Ralph. Walker was almost afraid to compliment his normally incompetent deputy for fear of a relapse.

Jack said to Mary, "Is there anything I can do for you?"

Mary, remembering how rude she'd been to him the last time they'd spoken, smiled slightly. "I wish I could think of something you could help with, but I can't. Thank you anyway."

Jack impulsively shook her hand instead of doing what he wanted to do—hug her—and ran to catch up with Ralph, who was impatiently gunning the motorcycle.

As they departed, they crossed paths with Mr. Prinney in his old Ford, chugging up the incline with headlights blazing.

"What's happened?" he said as he struggled hurriedly out of the car. "Jack Summer called my office to say that Mrs. Towerton needed help immediately. What's wrong?"

"Nothing," Mary said. "I'm sorry you were alarmed. Jack didn't need to get in touch with you."

"He said searchers were needed. I brought flashlights," Mr. Prinney said kindly. "Let's go inside where it's warm. Mrs. Towerton, you're only wearing a shawl. You must be freezing."

Mary went indoors and Walker held Mr. Prinney back on the porch and explained what had happened. "The note appears to involve you," he said, pulling it out gingerly and not allowing Prinney to touch it.

It had become dark enough by now that Mr. Prinney had to turn on his flashlight to read it. "What an ignorant person," he said. He gestured at the chairs on the porch for Walker to sit down.

Mr. Prinney didn't speak for a few minutes. Then he finally said cautiously, "You know I can't reveal any information about clients. But you should know that Mrs. Towerton consulted with me at my home office on the day Brother Good-heart's death was discovered. It had nothing to do with the preacher's death. It was a personal matter involving the welfare of her husband. Even that is more than I should say."

Walker thought for a moment. "You think who-ever wrote this note saw her coming to Grace and Favor with information about Goodheart's death?"

"Not necessarily. But it's a possibility you might want to consider. She came back later that day. And I visited her here later. That's all I can tell you."

"Thank you," Walker said, rubbing at his ear in consternation. "I need to go interview Joey."

"I'll be any help I can," Mr. Prinney said. "Be careful getting out of that chair. It wants to tip over. Mrs. Prinney is holding up dinner for me. I'll be on my way."

Walker remained in the rickety chair, consider-ing. So far in the case of the death of the radio minister, he hadn't dealt with anyone so badly educated to write such a note. Except maybe that slutty girl he and Lily interviewed, and he doubted she even had an automobile. He'd have to check on her anyway.

Did Mr. Prinney's theory hold water? he won-dered. It was obvious that Mrs. Towerton wasn't consulting with a lawyer about Pottinger's death. Wasn't it? Surely Mr. Prinney wouldn't have said anything about their meeting if that had been the case.

So it would seem Mrs. Towerton's visit was an unfortunate coincidence of timing. And somebody thought she was threatened by it.

"She," he'd thought. Who could "she" be? The girl Lily called Brunhilde? He'd spoken to her and she didn't seem especially bright. But maybe the person who wrote the note spoke perfectly good English and simply didn't know how to spell. He glanced again at the note. It wasn't ungrammatical, just badly spelled.

Maybe it wasn't really a woman. There were a few effeminate young men who considered themselves artists or Communists and who wore their hair long. Was the boy old enough to know for sure it was a woman?

He carefully rose from the chair, which *did* try to dump him out, and knocked at the door. "It's me, Howard Walker, Mrs. Towerton."

She called to him to come in. The little family was sitting at the table eating dinner. The little boy had his napkin tucked into the collar of his shirt. Mrs. Towerton was feeding the baby a mashed-up vegetable of some sort from a pretty bowl with a little enameled spoon.

"Would you like some stew, Chief Walker? I've made plenty."

"I would, thank you. It smells wonderful. Better than anything that's cooked at the boardinghouse."

The little boy was still eating his dinner, stuffing a biscuit in his mouth with an eye out that his mother didn't see him do it. Walker wouldn't question the boy until they'd all finished dinner.

When Mary put the baby in her little crib and started clearing the table, Walker said to Joey, "What are your favorite toys? Would you show them to me?"

Joey took Walker's hand and led him to a little trunk near the stove. Walker sat down next to him on the floor and admired the toys. While Joey ran a little cart over the pristine floorboards, Walker asked, "What did the woman who took you in the car look like?"

Joey shrugged. "Just a lady."

"What color hair did she have?"

Another shrug. "I dunno."

"Where did she drive to?"

"I dunno."

"What did you see when she drove?" Walker asked.

"Trees," Joey said, and added after screwing his face up to remember, "and a cow."

That was no help. Nearly everyone in the countryside hereabouts had at least one cow, even if they and the cow were starving. Next only to a radio, a cow was the last thing poor people let go.

Maybe he should test out one silly theory. "Joey, how did you know it was a lady? Could it have been a man?"

Joey laughed. "The lady had a dress."

"What color dress was she wearing?"

Joey thought for a minute or two. "I dunno. You run the wagon now."

Walker obliged by taking the toy and turning it in a figure eight, while asking, "What did the lady say to you?"

"I dunno. Nothing."

"Did she tell you to get in the car?"

"She open't the door and her hand do this," he said with a "come on in" gesture.

Thinking about the red and white monstrosity Mrs. White had bought for the minister, Walker asked one more question as he handed back the toy cart. "What color was the car?"

"This color," the boy said, holding up the cart, which had been painted black.

Great! Howard thought. Almost every car in town was black.

Apparently Joey cared deeply where each toy was put in the small trunk. "My daddy made me this. And this," he said, pointing out the brown-painted horse that pulled the cart.

After Walker helped Joey put his toys away, Mary said to the boy, "It's bedtime. See? Emily's already asleep. Give her a little soft kiss and put on your pajamas."

When Joey went to change in the other room, Mary said, "I'm sorry you didn't get any useful information from him. He's just a little boy. Children that age don't notice the same kind of things you and I would."

"Did anything he said mean anything to you?" Walker asked.

"No. It didn't. All I care about is that she brought him back. And I swear I'll never let him be outside again without me. I'm going to have a locksmith out. None of the doors have ever had locks. I never thought we'd need them."

Walker headed toward the door. "I'll send someone first thing Monday morning. Try to jiggle Joey's memory. Maybe he'll remember something helpful."

"I will. I promise. But I don't hold out much hope. Children's memories are very selective— they only remember things that are important to them. This didn't upset him in the least until I started hugging him and crying. He had no idea he was in danger. If you'd asked him about his ride in Jack's motorcycle a few months ago, he could tell you all about it in detail because it was exciting."

Chapter 21

The next morning, before Walker let Ralph take the note away to Chief Colling's pet fingerprinting expert, he copied it out, then wrote up a statement including the misspelled words. It read, *I went to the lawyer then purchased my groceries and brought them home and nobody tattled on me.* He wanted to keep the made-up message light so that nobody would feel threatened.

The fingerprint expert probably wasn't available on Sunday. Walker hoped Colling would still have him around again Monday.

Then he called the locksmith from Fishkill who'd installed the locks at Grace and Favor.

"I have another job for you. A woman who lives with her two little children. One of them was temporarily kidnapped. I want you to install locks on all her doors and windows first thing in the morning. Just charge her for the hardware. She works hard to support her children. I'll put in for your labor to the city budget for protection for a citizen. If they won't pay it, I will. Okay?"

"Howard, I made a good amount on those folks at the mansion. I'll only charge her for half the hardware and you the other half. No labor charges. Fair enough?"

Howard gave him directions to Mrs. Towerton's house, grateful that the locksmith was such a good person.

With these matters tended to, he took this revised version of the note on Joey's jacket to Susanna Cooper and Kathryn Staley.

Susanna opened the door, paled for a moment, and invited him in. Both women were wearing handkerchief bandannas around their heads. Susanna was holding a duster and Kathryn a large rag and a jar of what looked like vinegar. No wonder their home was so tidy. They probably did their cleaning every Sunday before going to church.

"I'm sorry to interrupt your cleaning, but I need you to sit at opposite ends of the room and write down what I say," he told them, handing each of them a piece of paper from his notebook.

"Why should we do this?" Kathryn said in her best Brunhilde shriek.

"Because I say so," Walker said firmly. "I can take you both to the jail to do it, if that's what you prefer. You can stay there as long as it takes."

Susanna paled but said, "Kathryn, we'll do as he says right now."

So she has a spine, Walker thought. Maybe she's really the dominant voice when she needs to be.

The two young women took chairs as far apart as possible. He told them to print the words rather than write in cursive, then read out the statement slowly. When they'd written down what he said, he took the papers carefully by the corners and put each in a separate envelope, already labeled with each name.

He thanked them for cooperating, got into his car, and drove down the road until he was out of sight before he pulled off on a side road and parked.

Gingerly, he pulled each effort out of its envelope to study it. Their printing didn't match the printing on the original note. However, anyone could disguise the way they printed, so that didn't matter much.

Susanna Cooper's was letter perfect: very neat handwriting, everything spelled right. Kathryn Staley's was tidy writing and she'd written the suspicious words correctly, but she'd spelled *groceries* as *grocerys*. He put the samples back in their envelopes and headed for Joan Wilton's home.

When she came to the door, she opened it only enough for him to see she was wearing only a skimpy nightgown that was grubby and frayed around the low neck.

"You're back. You'll have to wait your turn. Give me fifteen minutes."

"I don't think you understand why I'm here. I need you to write out something for me. We can do it here or I can take you to the jail for it just as you are."

"You bastard!" she sneered. "Let me get a coat at least." There was the sound of a man's voice raised in objection inside the house, then Joan Wilton appeared a moment later with a coat and scruffy slippers on. She sat down on a rickety bench by the door. "Let's get this over with."

Walker handed her a pencil and sheet of paper and his notebook to write on and read her the statement she was to print. When she was done, he took them back gingerly, holding the paper and the notebook by the corners. There might be fingerprints on them that could be useful.

Monday morning, Walker was a bit late getting to his office. Ralph had taken a call from Colling's fingerprint expert.

"He says this here piece of wrapping paper has really been around the block. Lots of fingerprints. Mostly smudged. None clearly belonging to anyone at the Institute. He noticed a tiny thread caught on the corner. Says it looks to him like a thread from a pair of black cotton gloves."

"Take these notes back to him. And my notebook. See if any of them can be identified."

When Ralph had left, Howard had to resist the impulse to bang his head on the desk. Of all the crimes he'd dealt with, this one seemed to him to be the most fruitless and frustrating. Chances were that he'd never solve this case, and it would ruin his so-far-perfect record of solving crimes.

To be perfectly honest with himself, he didn't

care very deeply who had killed Pottinger. He was an evil person who was simply out to rob the poor and downtrodden to line his own pockets. Who could guess how many other young women he'd taken advantage of in his life? He wasn't a loss to society, except to the people who'd worked for him.

Howard had no idea where to go, what to do next. If, by the remotest chance, any one of the fingerprints he'd just collected could be proved to match any of the ones on Joey's note, he might come out all right and get this case off his plate.

He seriously doubted it would work out that way.

While he was brooding over this, his phone rang.

Monday afternoon, Lily had to fulfill her promise to Mrs. Tarkington to call again on Miss Jurgen.

As she expected, Amelia Jurgen didn't know very much more about her renter than she'd already told Lily.

"All I know is that she didn't seem to cook much," Miss Jurgen said with a smile. "The same furnace serves both parts of the house, and I have a very good sense of smell. I suppose she ate elsewhere most of the time."

Shifting the conversation, Miss Jurgen said, "I just received a lot of payments for my patterns. Enough to get my car repaired. I'm going out back to see if I can make it work long enough to get it to the man who's supposed to be repairing it. If I can't get it rolling, I'll fix us something to nibble on."

Lily followed her to the big garage at the back of her long lot. There was another car in the garage as well that Lily assumed belonged to the renter. Miss Langston must have taken the train home. She watched as Miss Jurgen tried to get the car started. It ran for a moment, then coughed and died. Miss Jurgen tried a couple more times with the same result. Lily leaned back on the front of the other car and was surprised.

"Miss Jurgen, this engine is warm."

"It can't be. It's Miss Langston's car. I assumed she took the train to wherever she went. I supposed the only reason she'd come back was to fetch her car." She hopped out of hers and felt the front of the car.

"Someone's driven it lately," Lily said. "Think. Did you hear the garage door open recently?"

"No, but I wouldn't. I keep the hinges well oiled."

"I think you should call the chief of police."

"I'd hate to bother him with this. She probably just gave the car keys to some friend of hers to use while she was gone." Miss Jurgen thought about this a moment, frowning.

So did Lily. "Can you name three of her friends? Or even one? Miss Jurgen, if someone has her car keys, they might also have her house keys. You really should call Chief Walker."

* * *

"Chief Walker, this is Amelia Jurgen. I know you're probably very busy but I hope you can come to my house sometime soon."

"I can come right now. Give me your address."

Walker arrived just as Lily and Miss Jurgen came around the far side of the house, after checking that Miss Langston's entry door was locked.

They explained what they'd discovered. He didn't seem to take it very seriously. "You think someone is living in her part of the house?"

"Someone I don't know? Yes. And I don't feel good about that. Who knows who it might be."

"Let's check then. I presume you have a duplicate set of keys. Would you write a note authorizing me to go inside with you?"

"Of course."

She fetched the keys, wrote the permission note, and all three of them went into Miss Langston's part of the house by the side door.

"Don't touch anything," Walker warned the women.

Miss Langston must have had very simple tastes. For all Lily could tell, it was a vacant house, sparsely furnished. No pictures on the walls. No personal ornaments. No items left on the flat surfaces. No books. No radio. The bed was neatly made with fresh-smelling sheets and a bedspread. There was no makeup in the bathroom. No dressing gown. Just tooth powder, a toothbrush, a bar of soap, and a plain glass on the rim of the sink. A dry towel and washcloth were draped neatly over the edge of the tub.

Walker had a jackknife in his trouser pocket. He edged the drawers of the chest in the bedroom open rather than touching the knobs. One drawer held a sparse amount of underwear, one nightgown, and a cord and tiny wooden clothespins to hang the items out to dry in the bathroom when they were washed. Odd, he thought. He hadn't seen washing powder anywhere. Maybe she cleaned her clothing with the bar of soap. Another drawer held a sweater, a pair of women's trousers, and one neatly folded blouse.

The rest of the drawers were empty. "How old do you think this woman is?" he asked Miss Jurgen.

"Hmm. Probably thirty. Maybe late twenties. I saw so little of her that I never really thought about it. Why do you ask?"

Walker paused, forming a tactful reply. "Shouldn't a woman of childbearing age have other things in her bathroom?" he half mumbled.

Miss Jurgen wasn't as prissy as he. "Maybe she'd had a hysterectomy. Or more likely she took them along with her, wherever she went."

Walker nodded gratefully, then asked, "You say you shared a house and you never saw her?"

Miss Jurgen explained about their business arrangement and their living conditions.

"You were business owners and never saw or spoke to each other?" Walker asked.

"No. She was an employee. Piecework of a sort. We each had a door with a different lock to the common work area. She'd leave her designs on the worktable. I'd decide which ones to use and market them, sharing a part of the profits on the ones I liked. Do you want to see the room?"

"Maybe I should," Walker said. This was becoming yet another little mystery he ought to be able to solve. "Let's look over the kitchen first."

In the icebox, there was still a tiny bit of ice and the water had either evaporated or been emptied. But the icebox was a sturdy insulated wooden one that probably kept cold for a long while.

Inside was a loaf of bread that was quite dry. A small ham wrapped in waxed paper. Three apples. An orange. A brown banana. In the pantry there was only a small skillet that hadn't seen much use, a toaster, several dusty cans of soup and beans, and a box of stale crackers. In the shelf next to the sink there were two plates, two drinking glasses, one set of silverware, and three napkins, one slightly frayed and stained.

"I was telling Miss Brewster earlier that I thought Miss Langston seldom cooked," Miss Jurgen said. "What little is in the icebox is probably what she made for her lunches to take to school."

"Oh, a teacher. Is she the one you're substituting for?" Howard asked Lily.

"Yes, and she appears not to have gone to the home address she gave the principal." Lily said. "Mrs. Tarkington wrote to her when she first left, and the letter came back marked 'not known at this address' or some similar wording. So she found the telephone number for the address and called it. The people were elderly, knew everybody in the small town's business, and had never heard of her. Mrs. Tarkington thinks perhaps she put down the wrong town name."

"How could someone make that kind of mistake?" Howard countered.

"Maybe she'd lived in a lot of little towns and just mixed them up."

Howard considered this might be possible but was unlikely.

"It looks to me as if this place isn't being used. Do you agree?"

"I do," Miss Jurgen said. "She must have had other clothes and such that she took with her."

"Was it always so empty looking?" he asked. "No pictures on the wall? No books?"

Miss Jurgen shrugged. "I don't know. I never came in here after she moved in. I provided the basic furniture, the icebox, and stove. I never thought of asking what she'd done with her half and never invited her into mine. Let's go back to my side. I made some cookies this morning and can do some coffee or tea if you can stay. We can talk this over."

Chapter 22

The three of them talked only about how good the cookies were. Miss Jurgen insisted on sending a paper bag of them home with Chief Walker. He'd obviously liked them.

"The woman who cooks at the boardinghouse where I live and work prefers gummy, greasy undercooked tarts. Lily, do you need a lift home?"

"Are you going that way?" Lily asked.

"I could," he said.

As he opened the door of the police car for Lily, Amelia Jurgen watched out the front window, wondering if they were sweet on each other. It would be easy to like Chief Walker very much. She'd never had dealings with him but often saw him around Voorburg and had always thought he was handsome with that dark hair and slightly Indian-looking eyes.

When Howard dropped Lily off, he went back to his office and sat at his desk with his feet up on it and his chair balanced on the back two legs. He did his best thinking in this precarious position.

Miss Amelia Jurgen had interested him. She, like Mrs. Towerton, appeared to have carved out a successful, if not very exciting in his view, way to make a living by herself. Both had been fortunate enough to inherit a house of their own as well. As had Lily, come to think of it.

He occasionally thought how pleasant it would be to have a nice house of his own. In his imagination, there was usually a wife involved in the fantasy. No one in particular. There were lots of good choices. But he himself wasn't a good choice. His income probably barely exceeded by much either Mrs. Towerton's or Miss Jurgen's. Although the town had voted him a meager raise six months ago, which was encouraging. If the financial situation improved with Roosevelt in the White House, he might be blessed with another raise someday.

Switching mental gears, he thought he should have asked more about this mysterious Miss Langston. How and why did she and Miss Jurgen share a home without knowing or caring anything about each other? At least it had sounded like that, from Miss Jurgen's view. Two young women who lived in the same house and worked together should have had opportunities to learn a little bit about each other.

Was it Miss Jurgen's choice to keep a distance from her renter or Miss Langston's, or both of them? He suspected it was Miss Langston. Miss Jurgen hadn't seemed too shy or standoffish. And she and Lily seemed to be friends.

He ate one of Miss Jurgen's delicious chocolate cookies while he brooded aimlessly on the reason she'd called him. It was distinctly odd that Miss Langston had given the principal of the school a clearly wrong address. Thinking like a cop, who normally saw things in a logical way, he found that hard to figure out. How long had Miss Langston lived here in Voorburg? He should have asked. She could have deliberately given the school a fake address, but why would she?

He tipped his chair back upright and looked at his watch. It must be about time for school to let out. Since he wasn't getting anywhere with his investigation into Brother Goodheart's death today, he might as well have a talk with this Mrs. Tarkington.

He arrived at the school just as the children were being let out for the day. Mrs. Tarkington, he supposed it was, stood at the front door warning them all to go straight home so that their parents wouldn't worry about them. She seemed to be saying it by rote and the children pretty much ignored her.

The older ones sought out any younger brothers or sisters and hustled them along, pretending to ignore them. Pairs of girls held hands and swung their arms as they headed away. Bigger boys talked in whispers and laughed uproariously. Probably saying dirty, forbidden words to amuse each other. Kids getting out of school for the day hadn't changed much since he was a youngster, he supposed.

He was in uniform and the older woman at the door, having waved the children off, looked at him with concern. "I'm Mrs. Tarkington. The principal. Is there something wrong?"

"Nothing much. I'd just like to ask you some questions, if you have the time," he replied with a smile to allay her slight alarm.

She took him into her office and closed the door. "Ask away," she said, sitting behind her desk and gesturing for him to pull up a chair. "I always have a cup of coffee when the children are dismissed, to keep me from going home and taking a nap. Would you join me?"

"Gladly," he said, wishing he'd brought along a few of Miss Jurgen's cookies to share. "I'm just wondering about your missing teacher, Miss Langston. I was called to her house this afternoon because someone appears to have used her automobile recently."

"How could that be?" Mrs. Tarkington asked over her shoulder as she prepared two generous cups of coffee.

"That's what the woman she rents her house from was wondering."

"Isn't Miss Jurgen charming?" she said, handing him a hot cup of strong coffee and putting a little linen cloth on his side of the desk to set it on. "She comes once a year to school and shows the children what she does for a living. The boys are bored senseless and the girls love it. I always sit in because she's so enthusiastic about her work. I hope to instill the same feeling in the students of liking their work, whatever it might be when they grow up. Maybe I could talk you into speaking to them occasionally about your job?"

"You're in a job you love as well, it appears," he said. "As am I. But I can't count on being free any specific time."

"I'm flexible about schedules," she said. "I could fit you in whenever you have a little free time."

After this pleasantry, he came to the point. "After speaking with Miss Jurgen, who seems to be a bit alarmed by Miss Langston's car being used, I started wondering what you could tell me about this teacher."

"I know very little about her," Mrs. Tarkington said. "I took her in a fit of panic a year and a half ago when the man who was teaching the class suddenly took off for greener pastures. California, of course. Don't they all go to California when they're fed up with their life and families?"

"It seems so," Walker said mildly.

"I was desperate to fill the spot with almost anyone until I could shop around among my peers," she went on. "But I kept her on. She was a good teacher. The children didn't love her but they enjoyed their studies. That's the most important thing."

"I suppose she's made a lot of friends among the parents," he said.

"Not at all. As far as I can tell, she has no friends. You must have never met her?"

"I haven't," he agreed.

"She's—it's hard to explain—she doesn't seem to like adults. I don't know if they're a threat to her or simply don't interest her. She's bossier and more aggressive with them than with the children."

"Have parents complained about her?"

"Only a few. Most of them put up with her because they can tell she's doing a good job teaching their children. What irritates them is that she insists on seeing their homes. She has some theory that what they have in their houses tells you a lot about how they think and who they really are. Teachers and principals in small towns are often invited for dinners or visits. Especially if they're single or widowed as I am. But she doesn't wait to be asked. She just turns up. They think it rude."

"So do I," Walker said.

Mrs. Tarkington nodded in agreement. "What she does in her free time isn't, in theory, relevant to me. Unless, of course, it is something illegal or immoral. Rudeness isn't quite in that category."

"Are you the least alarmed that she seems to have gone missing?" Walker asked.

"A little bit," Mrs. Tarkington said. "She told me she had an appendix that flared up a bit from time to time. And that her lifelong doctor was moving away from her hometown and wanted to

get it out while she was well. It's possible something bad happened to her. I'd be more alarmed if
Miss and Mr. Brewster hadn't been willing to step
in and help out. They're delightful young people
and well educated. I suspect, however, that they
might not want to take up their jobs here forever
though."

It was interesting to Howard to see how well
focused Mrs. Tarkington was. It seemed the
whole rest of the population was fascinated with
and somewhat horrified by Brother Goodheart's
murder. She was probably the only citizen he'd
run into lately who didn't ask how the investigation was going. There wasn't any way she
couldn't know about it. But she stuck to what she
did well.

"Do you know anything about her previous life
or outside interests?" he asked, getting back to
Miss Langston.

"All I know is that it seems she eats her dinner
often at Mabel's Cafe. I go there from time to time
myself. Since I was widowed, I have very little interest in cooking for myself, you see. I think every
time I've gone there, Miss Langston was in the far
corner reading a book while she ate. The first time
I ran into her there, I asked if she'd like me to join
her and she said, 'No, thank you.' So I never tried
again."

"Did you ever see her eating with anyone
else?"

"Never. I'm sorry I can't be more help. If Miss

Jurgen is worried about staying alone in her house, I could offer to let her have my back room. Should I ask?"

"I think Miss Brewster will probably beat you to it. Grace and Favor has more rooms than anybody else. Miss Twinkle boards there, you know."

A light came into Mrs. Tarkington's eyes. "She does? How interesting. I thought she still lived over her millinery shop. I might talk to the Brewsters about myself. It's a bit lonely living alone. I didn't know they took boarders. It's an enormous house. It shouldn't surprise me."

"Isn't it though," Walker agreed. "I have to admit that's why I live at the boardinghouse and have my office there now—I hated living alone and cooking for myself. Besides, it was right next to the river and the trains."

He stood. "I appreciate your observations, Mrs. Tarkington. I won't take up any more of your time. I might just eat at Mabel's tonight though. I understand it's Irish stew night. Would you care to join me?"

She sparkled like the pretty girl she must have once been. "I'd be delighted! What time?"

Chapter 23

Howard went back to the boardinghouse after dinner, wondering what had inspired him to have the meal with Mrs. Tarkington. He guessed it was because she was not only straightforward and in control, but lonely as well. She'd be a lot happier living at Grace and Favor than living by herself. And the residents would probably like having her there. If Mrs. Tarkington didn't contact them soon, he'd probably mention the conversation to Lily and Robert.

Or maybe he shouldn't. He had no justification for butting in. Mrs. Tarkington wasn't shy. She'd obviously liked the concept of living with congenial people and not having to cook for herself.

He'd wasted his time trying to learn anything he didn't already know about Miss Langston at Mabel's. The waitress cringed when he mentioned her name. "That awful woman! She insists on always seeing if the kitchen is clean enough to satisfy her. I've never waited on her that she didn't complain about something. Soup too salty.

Bread too cold. Roast beef too tough. I don't know why she comes here."

"Has she been lately?" Walker asked.

The waitress tilted her head a little and thought. "I hadn't really noticed, but no. Not for a couple of weeks, come to think of it."

He decided when he returned home that he really didn't care what had become of Miss Langston. Apparently she wouldn't be missed by anyone. And since nobody had filed a missing person report, he wasn't responsible for finding her.

Meanwhile, the fact that he'd been considering a different case had cleared his mind of Brother Goodheart's death. All the picky details had fallen away, and now he could clearly see that only two of the four people most closely involved with the man were strong suspects.

Nobby Hazard was still first on his list. Nobby had wholeheartedly worshiped the fake preacher. If someone had told him convincingly that it was likely that Goodheart/Pottinger had a serious flaw in his nature, Nobby would have been fully capable of killing him out of sheer outrage. Nobby was a fanatic who'd met and worked hard for another fanatic. If the curtain behind which Pottinger concealed his real moral failings had been ripped away, it would have destroyed Nobby's entire view of him. He'd most likely feel he had to stop the man—dead.

Howard had no proof against him though. No

fingerprints, no physical evidence whatsoever. Just motives. None of those who were staying at Grace and Favor that Saturday night had an alibi except being alone in their own rooms overnight. The fourth suspect on his list, Big Jimmy Rennie, didn't have a provable alibi either. But he wouldn't have known which room Pottinger was in, or that the door was unlocked.

Howard's feeling about Nobby was a gut reaction, which he'd learned was usually reliable. But if he ever found the evidence to take Nobby to court, the judge and jury would wonder what a madman who should clearly remain locked up in the loony bin was doing in a courtroom.

All three of the guests were dependent on keeping Goodheart alive, kicking, bringing in the money, and providing them with jobs at a time when jobs of any kind were thin on the ground.

Big Jimmy Rennie most of all. He lived a very high life. A big house, a devoted wife, the best of suits, ties, automobiles, and dentures. If he'd fiddled the books as Goodheart was apparently claiming at the secret meeting, he'd be out of work. But the same applied if he'd knocked him off. However, all of Howard's real knowledge about Rennie's sense of honor had come, not from him, but from Rennie's wife.

Munching on another of Miss Jurgen's excellent cookies, Howard also suspected that Edward Price was also an unlikely suspect. Price had admitted he disliked the preacher intensely. But his high moral stance was colored by the fact that he stuck with the job. Another one who had nothing to gain and everything to lose by murdering his employer.

Jackson Kinsey, however, was probably better off with Goodheart dead. Kinsey was the executor of what was doubtless an enormous estate. There would be extraordinarily high fees coming to him for this. Apparently he was one of those individuals who was able to bounce back from committing civil and financial crimes.

At least Kinsey had good reason to stick around as long as he could drag the estate settlement out. The longer the legalities took, the more money he'd make. This mysterious son of Pottinger's youth, if he was meant to inherit, would probably end up with only enough money for a bus ticket home.

Why haven't I paid more attention to the son? Howard asked himself. Pottinger wasn't worth anything to his son alive. The boy may have thought his father would be much more valuable to him if he were dead.

How could I find him? Howard wondered. Nobody but Pottinger had ever seen or spoken to him. Nobody had any idea where he was or what he looked like. Not even what name he might be going by. That was an interesting thought.

Even Pottinger probably wouldn't recognize the small son he'd left behind in Nebraska if he turned up at the Institute with a different name and acquired a job as one of the toadies. Listening, watching, for an opportunity to bump off the old man.

There might be something in that.

His only other suspect was Brunhilde, a.k.a. Kathryn Staley. He felt sure she was in love with poor Susanna Cooper, and her beloved had been besmirched by Pottinger.

Again, he had no evidence to prove it. Lily had made good sense when she asked how Kathryn could have known which room he was in, and that the door wasn't locked. He wanted to suspect her first though, because he didn't like her, and second because she had a motive of passion.

He brushed the chocolate out of his teeth and went to bed, thinking of a list of things he should do the next day. Get in touch with the accountant in Albany who was studying Big Jimmy Rennie's bookkeeping. Call on Mrs. Taylor at the Institute to see if she could tell him anything more about Pottinger's son. Lastly, forget about the missing teacher. She wasn't his responsibility.

Howard hadn't needed to worry about Mrs. Tarkington. She went immediately from dinner with the Chief of Police to Grace and Favor. As her noisy little car pulled up in the driveway, she saw the place in a different way than she had on her other visit. It had merely been an enormous old house then—something that housed the people she needed to enlist for help. Now she looked at it as a potential home for her old age.

The noise of the automobile wheezing up the driveway had caught Lily's attention, and she met Mrs. Tarkington at the door. "Come in, come in," Lily said. "It's too cold to talk at the door. Is there something wrong? Have you heard from Miss Langston?"

Lily ushered the principal into the library.

"Nothing's wrong at all and, no, I haven't heard from Miss Langston," Mrs. Tarkington said. "I just had an early dinner with Chief Walker at Mabel's. He was asking about whether she often ate there, and happened to mention that Miss Phoebe Twinkle boarded with you."

"Indeed she does," Lily replied, wondering where this conversation was going.

"Might you like to have another boarder?"

"That depends on who it is, I suppose," Lily said.

"Me."

"You'd leave your comfortable house near the school?" Lily said with surprise.

"I could rent it out. It's not so dear to me now that my husband is gone. I'd like to rent or sell it to someone who could take better care of it. I'm not very good at dealing with periodic leaks in the roof and replacing windows that are too drafty."

"I'm sure we'd all love to have you here. Naturally, I'll have to consult with my brother and Mr.

and Mrs. Prinney, but I know they all like and re-
spect you."

"Then let's talk money, shall we?" she said
bluntly, smoothing her skirt down. "I'd want to
be fed without cooking for myself. I'd like to have
a room with my own bath, and enough space for
some of my own furniture. A warm room, too."

What she couldn't say to Lily was that she was
coming up on her sixtieth birthday and didn't
want to live alone and possibly die on a Friday
evening and be unnoticed until she didn't turn up
at school on Monday.

She went on, "Could I see some of the rooms
you have available?"

"There are many on the third floor. They're
small, though, and they don't have private bathrooms. It's a long walk," Lily said with a smile.
"But there are a few larger rooms on the second
floor."

Mrs. Tarkington stood briskly and said, "Let's
look at them. Nobody is committing to this yet.
That's understood, isn't it?"

"Absolutely."

Mrs. Tarkington took a deep liking to one particular room that Lily suspected had once been
Great-uncle Horatio's aunt Flora's. The furniture
was awful—old-fashioned and heavy. Luckily,
there were plenty of places it could be stored.

"Most of this is terrible," Mrs. Tarkington said
frankly, echoing Lily's thought. "But I love the
look of the big canopy-draped bed, and the

white marble fireplace. Might I pay extra to keep the bed?"

"Certainly you could keep the bed," Lily exclaimed. "But not pay for it. It would be a lot easier to leave it than move it. Nobody's used the room since we moved here. I don't know if it has enough large sheets, though."

"I can take care of that. Now, the bathroom is awfully dark. Could I hire someone to paint it a brighter color if I take the room?"

"Robert's turned into a fairly good painter, and I can't imagine anybody objecting to improving anything in here. I'd never even seen the bathroom until this evening. The Harbinger brothers are always looking for work as well."

"Speaking of it being evening, may I come up here tomorrow in the daylight and see the view?"

"Of course. It should be lovely. My own room is the second to the right of this one, and I can see the river from it."

Mrs. Tarkington shook Lily's hand and said, "I'll be on my way now. I'm not very good at driving in full dark. Talk to the others about it. And I'll give it a little more thought as well. Don't worry whether I can afford it, Miss Brewster. My husband left me fairly well off and I've been saving my own money for a long time. My dear William insisted that I keep my own income for myself."

Lily was pleased and assumed the rest of the residents would be as well. Mrs. Tarkington was certainly a respectable member of the community. She'd be good company, and they could use the extra income. Lily also suspected that Mrs. Tarkington was lonely living all by herself.

As the older woman was leaving, Lily said, "I've had another thought I've been meaning to share with you. If Miss Langston doesn't ever return, you might consider Mrs. Roxanne Anderson as a replacement. She's well educated and good with children. Almost all of her work on the vegetable garden is seasonal—a late-spring-to-early-fall job. She'd have the summer off to work on it. She probably needs a job, and her own children would be right there in the school with her."

Mrs. Tarkington smiled broadly. "I should have thought of her. Not that you and your brother aren't doing an excellent job. That's a good suggestion. Thank you, Miss Brewster."

Chapter 24

When Mrs. Tarkington had left, Lily asked Mrs. Prinney when dinner would be ready. "Do I have time to make a phone call?"

"Twenty minutes."

"I only need five."

Miss Jurgen had given Lily her phone number so they could set times when Lily could take some basic lessons in needlework. She put the call through.

Introducing herself, she asked, "I just wondered if you're all right?"

"I can't speak freely because the girl at the exchange is probably listening," Miss Jurgen said. "The man just came to tow my car—the *only* one in the garage."

"I see. Would you feel more comfortable here for a couple of days?"

Miss Jurgen laughed. "No. There are no automobiles in the garage now for someone to 'borrow,' and I've installed locks on the doors. I've had the hardware for nearly a year and it seemed a good time to use it."

"Good idea. I forgot to give you our number. I suppose the girl at the exchange knows it. Let me know when we can get together."

Neither of them sneezed but someone did.

Lily and Miss Jurgen said their good-byes and rang off.

There were three girls who handled the telephone exchange, and all but one of them always listened in for gossip. They traded off shifts and you never knew if you had one of the snoops or the nonsnoop, since their voices were so much alike. Sometimes the snooping was a good thing. If you had an emergency, the girls usually knew where the chief of police or Dr. Polhemus was.

Over dinner, Lily told everyone about Mrs. Tarkington's visit.

Mrs. Prinney was delighted. "How nice it would be to have a woman around my age to visit with." Then added as an apology, "Not that Lily, Phoebe, and Mimi aren't wonderful young women and delightful company for me."

"I thought we should charge her about twice what Phoebe pays for her room. Maybe even a little more. It's much larger and on the second floor, with two empty rooms on each side."

"Which room do you mean?" Robert asked.

"The one I think was Great-great-aunt Flora's,

or whatever relation she was. The one with the enormous canopy bed."

Robert groaned. "We don't have to haul that monster out, do we?"

"No, she wants the other pieces out so she can bring her own favorite furniture along with her, but she likes the bed. She wants to have the bath painted a nicer color."

"Who could blame her?" Robert said. "I looked in there once and it's worse than being in the basements."

"I think we should take a vote, if that's all right, Mr. Prinney. Of course, it's really up to you."

"No," he said. "Someday this will be your house entirely. I've only met Mrs. Tarkington two or three times at church and found her an admirable woman. I vote yes."

"Me, too," Robert and Mrs. Prinney said at the same time.

"Phoebe?"

Phoebe looked surprised. "I'm only a boarder. I shouldn't have a vote, should I?"

"I think from now on, everybody who lives here must have a vote," Lily said. "We all have to live together, eat together, and get along well. And the vote has to be unanimous. Mimi?"

"Mrs. Tarkington wasn't the principal when I was at school. She was a teacher and I liked her ever so much. I say yes."

The vote was unanimous as Lily expected. She

said, "We were both being terribly canny when we talked. Neither of us committed. She may have changed her mind."

"I hope not," Mrs. Prinney exclaimed.

Lily contacted Mrs. Tarkington right after they finished dinner. "Everyone agreed enthusiastically that we'd love you to live here. Our charge would be eleven dollars a month. That includes meals, cleaning, and washing of linens. Mrs. Prinney would even pack you a lunch." It was a dollar more than twice what Phoebe paid.

"I should tell you I'll think it over." Lily could hear the smile in her voice. "I won't, though. It's less than I feared. Much less for what I get, even aside from the good company. I can probably even afford to buy a more reliable car. Do you have a deadline of any sort?"

"No. That's up to you," Lily said. "Don't you still want to see it in the daylight?

"No, I'll trust that there's a good view. I'll get busy trying to rent or sell my house first thing tomorrow then."

The next day Chief Walker decided he needed at least one more talk with Mrs. Taylor at the Institute. He wanted to pry more out of her about this son of Pottinger's. He was barely out of Voorburg when he met with a roadblock. A truck full of hay had taken a corner too fast going north and shifted the load all over the road.

He took a detour onto a side road and noticed in passing that a big farmhouse that had been abandoned when the family took off for California had smoke coming out the chimney.

Someday when he had more free time, he'd check whether the family had come back or squatters had appropriated it. If it were squatters who were taking good care of it, they'd have to be informed they'd have to leave if the owners came back. If they were simply trashing it, he'd have to get them out.

He only had to drive two miles out of his way, so it was still early when he arrived at the Institute. He'd called ahead so that he'd be let in.

Mrs. Taylor greeted him and said, "Come in out of the cold. I have a fire going and strong coffee." As she led the way to her office, she said, "I've thought and thought about Pottinger's son. I think I already told you all I know about him, which isn't much."

"Do you know how long it had been since Pottinger had last seen his son?"

"Ages, I suppose." She thought for a moment. "I seem to recall one of the son's letters talking about his father leaving when he was only a year or two old. Of course, I gave the letters to Pottinger, so I can't check this. I doubt that he kept them. They were very unpleasant and accusatory."

Walker was silent as he took a sip of the coffee she'd served. It was so strong that he could probably have stood a spoon in it.

"I have a rather bizarre idea I want you to consider," he said, "and tell me if I've gone totally mad. You told me you thought the boy was nineteen or twenty. How did you know that?"

"I believe he said so in one of his letters. Probably the same one I just referenced. He said Pottinger had ignored him for eighteen years and it was too late to make up for the time and experiences lost."

When it came down to telling her his theory, it seemed even more harebrained to him. He'd come all this way to ask her, though, so he might as well just spit it out.

"I presume when people apply for a job, you don't require them to prove that they're using their real name. Birth certificates and such?"

"Lots of people don't even have birth certificates, and if they weren't christened, there's no way to prove they are who they say. We really had no need to know if they were using their real name, as long as they did a good job. But I know what you're thinking. The idea occurred to me as well. Had the son come here under a false name to get a job and decide whether he wanted to acknowledge Pottinger as his father? And if he disapproved of him, or actively hated him, he might have killed him, hoping he could claim his fortune. Isn't that what you're getting at?"

"Exactly. Of course, he'd have to change his appearance. Grow a mustache, dye his hair or something to keep from being recognized as a former employee."

"I think you said it was a bizarre idea. I thought so, too. But the more I think about it, the more likely it becomes. The problem, of course, is proving it. We hired a great many young men out of work over the years. Some didn't work out for long because they were incompetent to do their job. I don't recall that any of them even faintly resembled Pottinger. Of course, he could have taken after the looks of his mother's family. Going back to the problem of proof, how could you go about it?"

"Find out where in Nebraska they were, contact anyone there who remembers Pottinger, and ask if they remember what the boy looked like when he grew older. For all we know, when his mother died, some other family took him in. They might have a picture of him."

"How would you figure out what town it was to start a search?"

"Nobby Hazard might know, if they hooked up there. If not, I suppose someone could make a search of census reports of each county. It would be a huge job, but made slightly easier by the unusual name Pottinger."

"And who would do that research?"

"My budget doesn't allow it. But yours might."

"May I remind you that Jackson Kinsey is the executor and it's in his own best interest to drag this out as long as he can?" Mrs. Taylor said with a grim smile. "I wonder if the State of New York might step in?"

"It might. But that would take just as long. Imagine the years of red tape to get such a thing approved."

"You're thinking of giving up this idea?"

"I probably won't. A chief of police in a town where a brutal murder of a public figure has taken place can hardly just say he gives up. Much as I'd like to. To be perfectly frank, I don't care who did it as much as I care for my own good reputation."

"I understand that. My only suggestion is that you contact the people who took away all the paperwork the day his body was found, and ask them to try to find out if, by any chance, Pottinger had kept the letters. There's where I think I'd start. Or you could spend the time yourself going through the boxes."

"I can't stay in Albany that long. I'm in charge of the welfare of the people of Voorburg. As you say, Pottinger had no reason to save unpleasant letters. Most people wouldn't. But I appreciate you not throwing me out on my ear. I'll give it more thought."

Chapter 25

When Howard returned to Voorburg, the main road was still closed. So he took a few minutes to look over the vacant house he'd seen on the way up to the Institute. There was no longer smoke coming from the chimney. He found a back door that wasn't locked. The house looked like he hoped it would—nothing had been harmed. He walked through the rooms and found that no one was there.

Since he didn't have a search warrant, he didn't feel he should look into cabinets or closets. He'd have to drop by again when someone was there to warn them that they'd have to vacate if the owners returned.

He doubted they would. The owners of the house and small, narrow farm behind it were Yoast Gerrit, of long Dutch descent, and his pretty wife, Hildy. Howard had been called out to the house a year ago when Yoast had some of his farming tools stolen.

"I not only have no sons to help me, but now I don't even have my tools," he'd said.

That was probably what had caused them to move to California. Yoast often said to friends that Hildy was pretty enough to be in the moving pictures. Too bad they weren't still here to take a couple of the orphaned boys from the Institute to raise as their own and have the help they needed on the farm.

Mr. Prinney's secretary put his afternoon mail on his desk. He glanced through it and came to a return address reading "The Six Companies, Boulder City, Arizona."

He opened it carefully with a very sharp paper knife his wife had given him last Christmas.

Dear Mr. Elgin Prinney, Esq.

This is to notify you that I have identified the person you wrote to me about. The man referred to in the previous telegram as Rick Taughton was, in fact, Richard Towerton. Several of the men in the dormitory recognized him from the wedding photograph you enclosed. A new Death Certificate will be issued in the correct name and sent to his widow. I'm also enclosing a detailed account of where he's buried should Mrs. Towerton wish to place a headstone. We extend our sympathy to her.

I'm sending a copy of this letter to Mrs. Towerton as well as the picture you sent and burial plot information (Grave 6, lot 1, Boulder City Cemetery).

Best regards,
John Roberts
Superintendent of Housing for the Six Companies
cc: Mrs. Richard Towerton

Mr. Prinney folded it back into the envelope and told his secretary that he had an errand to run and would be back shortly. He drove out to Mary's house, thinking to himself that he was glad he hadn't actively encouraged her to think it was a mistake. After all, the telegram she received was properly addressed to her home in spite of having the wrong name. Poor Mary.

When he knocked on her door, she opened it holding her own copy of the letter.

"I'm so sorry, Mrs. Towerton," he said.

"I suppose I knew all along that it was Richard," she said. Her eyes were red but there weren't tears. "I'll write up an obituary for Mr. Summer to put in the paper now that it's official."

"Is there anyone else I could help you contact?"

"I can't think of anyone. Richard was an only child of only children for parents. There are no relatives that I know of. Except, of course, my children. Emily never knew him and I think Joey has forgotten him."

Mr. Prinney almost blurted out that now she could remarry. He caught himself before he spoke. This wasn't the proper time to say such a thing. It wouldn't be proper for him to mention it any time, in fact.

"They'll probably send the death certificate to my office," he said. "I'll bring it to you as soon as I receive it."

Jack Summer was standing at his office window, wondering idly when they'd be getting some snow. The farmers hereabouts needed the water for their fields. As he was gazing out, he saw Mary Towerton's wagon. She didn't appear to have the children with her today. She'd probably left them with a neighbor to do her grocery shopping. As he watched, she stopped in front of the newspaper office.

Good Lord! Was she coming to see him? He went to the door with a smile, wishing he had on better clothes and had combed his hair.

"Mrs. Towerton. How good to see you. Please come in. Forgive the mess my office is in."

She didn't smile back. She handed him a neatly written note. "This is my husband's obituary. I'd like it to be in the newspaper."

"Obituary?" he repeated stupidly. "I'm so sorry."

"So am I," she said. "Thank you," she added, heading for the door.

He caught up with her and put his hand on her shoulder before she could touch the doorknob. "You must be devastated by this news. Is there anything else I can do to help you and the children?"

She whirled and threw herself into his arms, sobbing. Suddenly she realized to her horror what she'd done and pulled away, deeply embarrassed.

"That's just it," she said through her tears. "I'm *not* devastated. Poor Richard." She pulled a handkerchief from the pocket of her coat and dabbed her eyes. "I'm sorry I've behaved so badly. I must go now."

Jack called Grace and Favor. Mrs. Prinney answered the phone. "Mrs. Prinney, Mrs. Towerton was just here to leave her husband's obituary to print in the paper. I thought you'd want to know."

"Oh, no! The poor darling girl, and those two orphaned children. I was just making a casserole to cook for dinner. I think I'll make another and ask Mr. Prinney to drive me right over there. Maybe bring some candies for her little boy. How did her husband perish?"

"The obituary says he died of pneumonia," Jack said. "I suspect that's not true. He was probably killed by falling rocks while digging the tunnels through the mountain. He was working at Hoover Dam. I guess you knew that."

"I didn't know what dam he was working on. Why would they lie?"

"Because if it's their own fault, they'd probably

have to pay death benefits. If it's a natural death, they don't. The last thing they want is bad press as well."

"Oh dear. How awful. I must call Elgin."

Chief Walker came to the door as Jack was hanging up the phone. "Jack, do you happen to know Yoast Gerrit and his wife, who lived in that house at the top of Lilac Road?"

"I don't think so. I've only been along Lilac Road once, when Highway 9 was closed. Why do you ask?"

"I was hoping you knew where they'd gone. There's someone living in their house. I thought I should tell them about it if I could, so they could let me know what they want me to do about it."

"Someone living there? Who?"

"I have no idea. There wasn't anyone in the house when I dropped by. I should have asked the neighbors about it while I was up there." Walker turned to leave.

Jack said, "Mrs. Towerton was here a few minutes ago. She was leaving the obituary for her husband to print in the paper."

"Oh, no! Poor lady," Walker said. "I knew she'd seen Mr. Prinney about something relating to her family. I should have guessed what it was. I'll drop off some toys for her children later."

"Mrs. Prinney's already making a casserole."

Walker smiled. "Of course she is. I guess I ought to pick up a roast or something as well."

Finding pork roast wasn't easy. Nor was finding toys. His landlady managed to unearth a well-used plush rabbit missing one ear that a former tenant had left behind. The baby wouldn't mind it missing an ear, Walker assumed. Mabel rummaged around in the lost-and-found closet at the restaurant and located a little metal policeman figure some child never reclaimed.

Walker headed out for the Towerton house and was surprised and pleased to see that a number of cars were parked in front. The word of Mary's husband's death must have spread like a wildfire. She obviously meant a good deal to a lot of her neighbors.

There were more casseroles and bowls of potato salad than he'd ever seen in one place. Many of the neighbors, knowing all that food wouldn't keep in Mary's small icebox, were eating what the others had brought.

Baby Emily latched onto the rabbit with glee and held it up to her cheek while she sucked the thumb of her other hand. Joey took the figure with a smile and said, "Is this you? Is it my birthday?"

Mary was being a good hostess, dragging out chairs and benches and washing up every dish as it was finished so someone else could use it. She only had six of them. Mrs. Prinney was still there, snatching away plates as people took their last bite. As Howard Walker handed Mrs. Towerton the little paper-wrapped pork roast, she said, "Chief Walker, you and Mrs. Prinney were the only ones so far who thought about the children. Thank you for that and for getting the locksmith out so quickly."

"It's the least I could do. I'm so sorry for your loss," he said. "If there's anything else I can do for you, just ask."

"I'm fine. Really."

"Well, I am glad to hear that. And now I think I'd better get out of the way."

"Aren't you going to have dinner? This is too much food for us to ever eat."

"I'd be glad to. I'll hold on to my plate with one hand to keep Mrs. Prinney from snatching it away."

Mary smiled.

"Chief Walker!" Mrs. Prinney exclaimed later as he was leaving. "My husband left me here. Could I have a ride home with you?"

On the way home, Mrs. Prinney said, "Poor girl. What is she going to do without a husband?"

Walker said, "She's survived a long time without a husband very well. She'll keep on doing well, I imagine."

Chapter 26

Thursday morning, Mrs. Tarkington took Lily aside as the children were arriving at school. "I had a chat on the phone with Mrs. Rismiller, the minister's wife, early this morning about changing the rotation of the flower providers for the church. She mentioned in passing that their son was moving back home to Voorburg."

"Oh dear. I understand he has very odd theories of religion."

"Yes, he certainly does. The point is, even though his mother didn't come right out and say so, they're in despair at the thought of having him in their home, pontificating to them about how wrong they are to believe as they do. Especially now, when that awful radio preacher has just been murdered. He seems to be closer to Brother Goodheart's philosophy than his father and mother can tolerate."

"I wouldn't blame them," Lily said. Then she opened her eyes very wide with alarm. "You didn't suggest him as one of our boarders?"

This made Mrs. Tarkington laugh. "No, of course not. I wouldn't want to be around him either. I told her I was thinking of renting out my house. She nearly fell at my feet in gratitude. They'll pay the rent themselves to house him, so he has no choice."

She went on, "The problem is that he's arriving next Monday. So I have to be out before that."

"Is that possible?" Lily asked.

"Only if I can catch the Harbinger boys before tomorrow. If I can, I wonder if you could cover for me at school tomorrow? I need to find a great many boxes for my belongings and decide which furniture I'm taking with me. I'm sorry to impose on you, but this is a golden opportunity I can't afford to miss. If a parent shows up, find out what they need. If it's vital, I'll come back to school."

Lily nodded. "I understand you hurrying. There aren't very many people around here who could afford the rental, and you wouldn't want the house to remain empty. I'll call Robert, if I may. I need to take his afternoon duties anyway so he can help supervise the move. The Harbinger boys will have to remove the things that are already in the room before your furniture will fit in.

"Oh dear," Lily added. "There's one thing we didn't work out. I think we should pay for moving the furniture out of the room, and you should pay for moving yours in. Does that seem fair?"

"I'd assumed that's how we'd do it. Please call

Mr. Brewster right now, if you would, to get it under way. I'm so thrilled at the way this has worked out so well, but it will all go for naught if we can't get the Harbinger boys. The Rismillers will need to have time to move a bit of their own furniture into the house before he arrives."

It took almost all day Friday for Mrs. Tarkington to pack up her valuables and for the Harbinger brothers and Robert to move out the hideous, heavy furniture in Great-great-aunt Flora's former room. The Harbingers arrived late in the afternoon at the principal's house with their truck to take the first load up to Grace and Favor. There were three heavy trunks, one holding her set of china, all carefully wrapped, and the second with most of her clothing and coats. The third and heaviest was filled with her books.

First thing Saturday morning, the boys were back for her furniture and the boxes that contained her sewing machine and the contents of her drawers as well as her bookshelves. She rode in the truck with them, clutching her jewelry case.

When the furniture was put where she wanted it, she closed the door and set about distributing her belongings.

"Do you need help?" Lily asked after knocking at the door.

"No, thank you. I'll have it shipshape before dinner."

"Would you like your lunch sent up on a tray?"

"Oh, my dear Miss Brewster, that would be a great help."

An hour before dinnertime, Mrs. Tarkington went in search of Lily. "Would you like to see the— *my* room?"

She'd transformed it into an elegant vision. Her little oval desk with her typewriter was next to one of the windows. An equally lovely small table was at the other window with her sewing machine. Her trunks were lined up at the far wall next to the bathroom door to be stored later in the vast basement of Grace and Favor. Her ivory-trimmed jewelry box sat in solitary splendor on a small round walnut stand in a corner of the room. Her oak bookshelves were filled with books and pretty ornaments.

Lily exclaimed, "I never imagined how large this room was and how beautiful it could become."

Mimi was right behind Lily with her dustcloths and carpet sweeper. "Oh, Mrs. Tarkington, this is so lovely. It will be a joy to clean. Could I start with the rugs now? They're a bit scuffed up by that big old stuff sitting and crushing them all this time."

"Could it wait until tomorrow, Mimi? I need a bath and to dress for dinner."

Mimi agreed to the plan and took away her cleaning materials.

"We don't dress up for dinner except on Sunday," Lily said. "We're usually informal."

"I shall dress tonight anyway. It's a day for celebrating."

Mrs. Tarkington was the last to appear for dinner. Everybody was stunned. She wore a long black georgette and silk dress with her hair piled up and a lovely diamond necklace and matching earrings. Howard Walker had been invited to dinner as well. Both he and Robert leaped up to escort her to her chair.

"You look like a princess, madam," Robert said.

"More of a dowager princess, I suspect," she said with a smile. "My late husband always liked to eat dinner with great formality. I haven't worn this dress since he passed over."

Mimi brought in the food and sat at her usual place. Mrs. Tarkington seemed not the least surprised that the maid ate with the family.

Mrs. Tarkington, sitting close to Mrs. Prinney at the end of the table, said, "Those potatoes were browned in the roast drippings and baked, weren't they? They look wonderful."

Mrs. Prinney almost became weepy. "It's so good to know my cooking is appreciated."

Lily managed to have a private conversation with Howard Walker after dinner. They went to the Yellow Parlor, which was seldom used.

"I want to thank you for getting rid of those reporters and turning away the religious folks,"

Lily said. "We haven't had another one turn up for two days in a row. Howard, I know it's really none of my business, but I wonder what more you've learned about the preacher's death."

"Nothing," he said glumly. "The more time that passes, the less I'm going to find out. My best guess, and it's only a guess, is that the killer was Nobby Hazard. He's the only suspect who's mentally unstable enough to have done it. That doesn't mean he did. I don't think I'll ever find proof."

"I'm sorry to hear that. What about the other case?"

"What other case?"

"The missing teacher," Lily said.

"I don't think of that as a criminal case. She took off for her own reasons. Nobody I've talked to knows anything about her past. Just that nobody except the children could stand to be around her."

"You're not going to give up on the preacher's murder, are you?"

"Clearly not. I can't afford to give up. It would be a serious blot on my reputation. He was a national figure, loved or hated by hundreds of thousands of citizens. No cop in the country who cared about keeping his job could afford to let it go. Keep this under your hat, will you? He has a grown son. I'm trying to find where and who he is."

"A son? How did you find that out?"

"Mrs. Taylor at the Institute told me about him. She's been opening the incoming mail for years and distributing it to the proper person. Pottinger seems to have kept track of where his son was, but he's not alive to tell us how he knew. The son's letters to him indicate that he hated his father."

He went on to explain the details of the son's end of the correspondence and the theory he and Mrs. Taylor had both come up with independently.

"I know it sounds crazy and desperate. Nobody has the financial resources to hunt him down. And the one person who's now in charge of his fortune, his attorney, doesn't have any incentive to find him."

Lily thought it over. "I don't think it's crazy. Who, except Nobby, would have a better motive according to what you've told me? Is there any way Robert or I could help?"

"I don't see any way anyone could, unless Pottinger kept the letters and they turn up in the material that was carted up to Albany. But you might know something else I'm trying to pursue. Have you ever driven up Lilac Road just north of here?"

"I don't think so."

"There's a house there that was abandoned and someone's living in it. I need to contact the owners and find out who's living there. I'd hoped someone in town knows where they went."

"Tell me their name and a little bit about

them and where their house is. I'll see what I
can find out."

"He was a farmer named Yoast Gerrit. An old
Dutch name. The wife was much younger and
very pretty. Named Hildy. I was called out there
once when someone robbed some of his tools
from the barn. I hear they went to California." He
explained how to find the house he meant.

"Exactly what do you want me to do?"

"Simply go to a couple of the neighbors to ask
if any of them have heard from the Gerrit family
and have their address. Ask, while you're at it, if
they've noticed who is living at the Gerrits'
house."

"I'll ask tomorrow at the meeting of the Voorburg Ladies League if any of the women knew
them."

Chapter 27

At the Voorburg Ladies League meeting Monday afternoon, Lily suggested inviting Miss Amelia Jurgen to join the group to replace poor young Ruby Heggan. Though Ruby was five months pregnant, her husband, Louis, had insisted on taking her and their baby girl all the way clear to California in his beat-up truck.

The group was delighted to approve Miss Jurgen. "I don't believe any of us know her well," Edith White, the founder, said. "Do you, Lily?"

"Fairly well."

"Would you like to be the one to extend the invitation?"

"I'd be glad to."

Tuesday afternoon, Lily dropped in on Miss Jurgen and said, "The Voorburg Ladies League would like you to join them."

"How nice of them. I'd be glad to. A year ago I wouldn't have had the time, but my business is doing so well now that I'm turning into a hermit. I need something to do outside my home once in a while now that my automobile is functioning."

"Well then, how would you like to take me for a ride today? Chief Walker has asked me to look at a house up on Lilac Lane to see if any of the neighbors know who's living in it. But I don't have a way to get there. It's such a lovely day outside for a change."

"Let's do that. Where is Lilac Lane?"

"Right off Highway 9 north of Voorburg. He gave me directions."

Miss Jurgen unlocked the garage door and they took off. Lily found the house easily. They pulled off the road a little short of it so they could look it over. As they were standing outside considering which other house to go to first, another car going the opposite direction stopped and pulled off the other side. An older woman stepped out of her car and approached them.

"Could you help me? I seem to have taken a wrong turn. I'm Mrs. Taylor and I have some paperwork that was delivered to me instead of Chief Walker and I need to get it to him in Voorburg."

Lily said, "Mrs. Taylor, we're friends of Chief Walker and doing a little job for him as it happens. I can give you directions. He's mentioned you to me, in fact. I have a map."

She fished it out of Miss Jurgen's car and they were studying it on the hood when Lily spotted a car coming from around the back of the house she'd been sent to look at.

Lily pointed to it and said to the other two women, "If it turns this way, see if you can tell who's driving it."

The car did indeed turn in their direction and slowed to squeeze between them. Mrs. Taylor said, "I can hardly believe it. That was Mildred Waywright. She worked at the Institute."

Miss Jurgen frowned. "No. It was Millicent Langston. She's my employee who shares my house and has gone missing."

"I'm afraid you're mistaken. I knew Miss Waywright fairly well. I'm certain it was she."

"I believe you are the one who is mistaken," Miss Jurgen said. "I know her extremely well and it was her car."

Lily was afraid they were going to seriously argue over this endlessly. She said, "Chief Walker must be told immediately. Mrs. Taylor, let us turn around and then follow us. We'll take you to Chief Walker."

Miss Jurgen and Lily got in the car and headed back toward Voorburg, with the mystery woman speeding far ahead of them and Mrs. Taylor right behind them. "I'm sure she's wrong," Miss Jurgen said as she drove. "That was clearly Millicent Langston."

"I suspect you're both right," Lily said. "Do hurry."

"What do you mean?"

Lily didn't explain. "Maybe we should follow her to see where she's going before we go to Howard's office at the boardinghouse."

They debated this for half a mile, but the car they were following sped up over the next hill and disappeared. "She's turned off somewhere," Lily said. "Let's go directly to Chief Walker."

The three women stopped at the boarding-house and ran inside. "Is Chief Walker here?" she asked his landlady.

"I think so. Go on up."

He was on the phone to Albany and was surprised to see the three women burst in together. He said to the accountant, "I'm going to have to call you back in a moment."

Hanging up, he asked, "What are all three of you doing here?"

They all tried to speak at the same time. He held his hand up. "Stop. One at a time."

Mrs. Taylor went first. "The people in Albany found copies of Charles Pottinger's letters and sent them to me by mistake. I was bringing them to you and became lost on the way. I asked directions from these two ladies." She gestured at Amelia Jurgen to speak in turn.

"We saw someone driving away from the house you asked Miss Brewster to look at," Miss Jurgen said. "It was Millicent Langston."

"No, it wasn't," Mrs. Taylor said almost angrily. "It was Mildred Waywright."

Lily stepped in and held her hand up to speak. "It was both, Howard. They're the same woman."

He grasped immediately what she meant. "Where did she go?"

"She was ahead of us," Lily said, "and must have dodged us on a side road over a hill."

Chief Walker summoned Ralph Summer. "Ralph, get in your motorcycle immediately. I'm putting Miss Jurgen on the phone with directions to her house. Don't do anything when you get there. Just park a house or two away until I arrive."

Miss Jurgen told Ralph how to find her house and gave the license number of Millicent's car. While she was speaking, Walker was writing something on his notepad.

When she hung up, he said to Miss Jurgen, "I need you to sign this. It says you're willing to give me your house keys. And that you authorize me to enter any part of the house you own."

Miss Jurgen signed it and said, "The extra keys are in the first drawer on the left in the table by my front door."

"Ladies, go to the jail and wait for me," he said as he ran out the door of his office.

"Jail?" Mrs. Taylor asked. "What is this about? Are we under arrest and supposed to turn ourselves in?"

"No," Lily said. "He'll want you both to identify her."

"You're going to have to explain this to me," Mrs. Taylor said, still miffed.

"I think that's going to have to be Chief Walker's job. Let's do as he said."

Mrs. Taylor had been convinced the other two women were lunatics until she realized that Chief

Walker had taken them seriously. She'd talked to
him enough times to realize he was perfectly
sane.

"I'll drive us to the jail, ladies. No need to use
up gas in two vehicles," she said pleasantly.

On the way, Miss Jurgen asked Lily, "How did
you make the connection?"

"It simply came to me that people who don't
know me well often call me Lil or Lillian, Lila or
even Lola. I've learned to answer to anything that
starts with an *L*, so it was a short leap from Mildred to Millicent. If you're going to go by a different name, it would be easier if the other name
started with the same letter and sounds close."

"That's clever of you. It makes sense, too," Miss
Jurgen said.

"There's something else tickling at the back of
my head," Lily said. "Would you mind dropping
me off at the grade school? I'll walk from there to
the jail. I need to ask one of the children something important."

"Mrs. Tarkington," Lily said to the principal,
"would you pull Bob out of class so we can talk to
him? I think he'll be more frank if you ask him
what I need to hear from him."

"What do you need to ask?"

Lily explained.

Mrs. Tarkington went to Robert and asked if
she could interrupt for a moment. She needed to
talk to Bob in her office.

The sullen boy who drove his father's truck looked alarmed.

When the three of them were closeted in Mrs. Tarkington's office, she said, "The morning after the death at Grace and Favor, Miss Brewster noticed that your classmates seemed to be sharing some secret. You appeared to be the source of the secret. You must be honest and tell us now what it was."

Bob hemmed and hawed and tried to convince them that he didn't remember, but Mrs. Tarkington gave him a look that only school principals do so well.

He caved in and told them, ending with "Hiram was with me."

"Thank you, Bob, for being honest with us. You may go back to class," Mrs. Tarkington said.

When he was gone, she turned to Lily, "What on earth . . .?"

"You're going to have to wait until dinnertime before it's explained," Lily said. "I must pass this along to Chief Walker."

Chapter 28

When Chief Walker and Ralph unlocked the door to the rented half of Miss Jurgen's home, the woman they were seeking threw a fit.

"Who are you? How dare you enter my house!"

"I'm the chief of police and we're here to arrest you for the murder of Charles Pottinger."

She had a suitcase in her hand, already heading for the door with the last of her belongings. She flung it at him, the corner of it striking his ribs.

She was like a rabid wildcat, hissing, spitting. She struggled to get through the door and run away, shouting obscenities. Both men could hardly subdue her.

When Walker finally managed to grab both her wrists, he said, "Ralph, handcuff her."

Ralph had been longing desperately to get to put handcuffs on someone, and he didn't do it especially gently.

As they wrestled her out the door, she suddenly became ominously calm and said quite firmly to Ralph, "You. Boy. Bring my suitcase."

"No, ma'am. Someone will fetch it later," Ralph replied with a grin.

When they reached the jail, she went haywire again when she saw Miss Jurgen and Mrs. Taylor from the Institute. She screamed, "So it's you two bitches who have done this to me. You'll be sorry. I promise you that!"

When she'd been safely put in the cell, Howard asked both Miss Jurgen and Mrs. Taylor to confirm that they knew her and to state the names under which they'd known her. He wrote up several papers and asked Ralph to take Mrs. Taylor and Miss Jurgen and the papers to Mr. Prinney to have the documents signed and notarized.

"Then tell your cousin Jack he can interview her. I want to hear what she has to say to the press."

Lily turned up a little later.

"I have something very important to tell you," she said. "Come outside where we can talk privately."

He followed her outside. "What is it?"

"The day Pottinger came to see me about renting the space, two of the boys in my class, one of whom can drive his father's truck, came up after school to see where we lived. But they saw Miss Langston's car parked near the gatehouse and decided they didn't want to run into her."

Lily went on. "My guess, and it's only a guess, is that she spotted Pottinger getting off the train, or driving through town."

"Either is possible," Walker said. "Go on."

"So the morning after Pottinger was murdered, the kids at school were all whispering to each other. I'd forgotten all about it until a little while ago. The boy in my class apparently took a friend back late that Saturday night to gawk again at where Robert and I live. He's admitted this, and his friend backs him up."

"They saw something?" Walker's eyes lit like beacons.

"They saw the car belonging to their missing teacher. Boys that age know every vehicle in town. That time it was parked in the woods. So they left the truck hidden as well, and sneaked up to the house and circled it. They saw Miss Langston going in the dining room windows. Neither wears a watch, but they thought it was about eleven or eleven-fifteen."

Howard said, "How did she know the house? How would she have guessed which room he was in?"

"That's the easy part," Lily said. "At the last Fate she demanded a tour of the house. She was, as you probably know, noted for her theory that you could tell a lot about people by seeing how they lived.

"Ask Phoebe about this. Ask Mrs. Tarkington," Lily went on. "I refused to let her talk me into showing her the house, or even to let her come inside to use the bathroom. I didn't even know her and didn't have the time or inclination to show her around. A little while later, she asked Robert if he'd show her around. He refused, and then she tried the same trick. She said could she simply go in and use the facilities. He let her. He went back to working at the Fate. Nobody knew how long she was there. She obviously took her own tour. And the master suite is the obvious place to house a group of men."

"How would she have known the door was unlocked?" Walker asked.

Lily smiled. "She didn't. But as you said to me, there are such things as lock picks. And she's exactly the sort of person who would have one handy. Didn't she have a handbag? Have you searched it yet?"

Walker looked deeply embarrassed.

"I guess I'm going to have to call the asylum and tell them to let Nobby Hazard go," he complained.

Lily went back to the school to see if she could catch a ride home with Robert.

Jack Summer turned up at the jail moments later, eyes bright as a squirrel's. "Ralph says you've caught the perp. May I interview her?"

"That's exactly what I want you to do. Hint to her that she needs to tell the world her side of the story. Be as sympathetic as you can. I'll be out of sight but listening and we'll both take notes of what she says."

Walker opened the door to the hallway where the jail cell was, being very careful not to be seen.

He left it open and sat down at his desk. He listened as Jack's footsteps sounded down the hall, then stopped.

"Who are you?" Miss Langston asked nastily.

"I'm Jack Summer, miss," Jack said in a low, pleasant voice. "I'm a reporter and I think you should tell the public your view of how you've been treated."

Walker had judged her correctly. She couldn't wait to explain herself in the best possible light.

"I worked for Brother Goodheart at the Institute of Divine Intervention. It wasn't a good job, but I believed so strongly in his principles that I didn't mind. I was asked to work with the children in the orphanage on the grounds."

Jack nodded sympathetically. "Go on."

"I discovered quite soon that he didn't want me to teach them anything but how to make the collection boxes faster. I realized then that he wasn't the good man I'd believed in so strongly."

"That must have been a shock," Jack said.

"It certainly was. I went to the main building and asked where he was. I was told he was in his bedroom and I could see him later in his office. Of course, I'd looked over the whole place at one time or another and I knew exactly where his bedroom was. I went straight up and told him what I thought of him."

"He must not have liked that," Jack replied.

"Not at all. He became violent. He started striking me."

"No!" Jack pretended to be shocked.

"It's worse yet. He raped me. Violently. Then just walked out of the room. When I finally got my wits back, I sneaked out a back way that not many people knew about and drove back to my apartment in Newburgh."

"Why didn't you go to the police or a hospital?"

"I've never trusted police or doctors. Neither group likes women. Or believe them. I wanted my own revenge. I'm very patient. I knew I'd get a chance to do something awful to him someday. Before I could figure out what to do to him, I discovered that I was pregnant."

"Oh, my! How upsetting that must have been," Jack said.

In the other room, Walker was writing furiously. He couldn't have been as good as Jack was at getting her to confess.

"It was. But after a little while, I realized it was *my* baby, too. I wanted to raise her."

"How did you know it would be a girl?"

"I just knew! A woman knows these things. But a month later I had a miscarriage and the doctor told me I'd never have another child. That was when I decided he had to die. He'd not only stolen my virtue, he'd stolen my chance of ever having a daughter."

Howard rolled his eyes and thought that was a good thing.

Miss Langston, as Howard thought of her, was still talking. Louder and faster.

"So I started spying on him. Waiting along the road to see where he went. Pretty soon I ran out of money and had to take a job here as a teacher. That made it harder to follow him. When I saw him one evening being driven through town in that big red and white car of his, I followed him to Grace and Favor. I hurried to the door and overheard him talking to that stupid girl who lives there. I knew when he was planning this meeting."

"That was clever of you," Jack said, nearly choking on the words he was having to say to this horrible woman.

"I made up a story about going home and kept an even closer eye on him. I knew his habits. I knew he always took a good long bath late at night. And I knew the layout of Grace and Favor. I had a good idea of what room he'd be in. I got some tools I thought I could use to fiddle the lock, if there was one. But the door opened at my touch. He looked so revolting in the bath. Leaning over washing his face, his big white back to me. I stabbed him and held his head under the water. I'm not sorry at all. He was an evil man. I've righted a great wrong."

Jack hardly knew what to say next. He could no longer pretend sympathy. He merely asked her, "Why did you kidnap Mrs. Towerton's son?"

"Kidnap? I didn't kidnap anyone. I don't know what you mean. When are you going to publish my story?"

That callous remark made Jack think for a second that he wouldn't publish it at all. But his reporter's instinct told him he must. He owed it to himself. He owed it to the public to reveal what kind of man Brother Goodheart had really been.

The revelations of what had happened that afternoon took all of dinnertime to explain.

Most of the residents of Grace and Favor were appalled, mostly by the fact that it was a woman who had committed such an act of brutality.

All but Mrs. Tarkington, who said, "I always said she couldn't get along with adults. I just never knew how truly hostile she could be if she set her mind to it."

"Why did she kill him?" Phoebe asked.

Howard Walker had naturally been invited to dinner to explain. He put his answer as tactfully as he could. "Because she said he attacked her sexually and she found that she was pregnant, then lost the baby. I suspect she didn't lose it accidentally, but she wouldn't admit that to Jack. She's presenting herself as the only injured victim."

Lily asked, "Why was her car in Miss Jurgen's garage that day you came over to look over her portion of the house?"

Walker shrugged. "For some reason, she was under the impression that Miss Jurgen wasn't home at the time. She wanted to reclaim the rest of her belongings. Or steal the pots and pans, for all I know. And that's why she came back again today.

"And, Lily," he went on to say, "I took your suggestion and went through her handbag. She had a bunch of little tools, tiny pliers, manicure scissors, and such, that she must have thought she needed to unlock the door to the suite. She'd have been smart to throw them away when she found out she didn't need them."

Phoebe had another question. "Was she the woman who took Mrs. Towerton's child as well?"

"She denies it. Though I'm certain she was," Walker said. "She has the idea that murdering Pottinger was justified in her warped opinion. But not even she can sound noble if she admits to kidnapping a child. I'm trying to figure out a way to let Joey see her, but not vice versa. I couldn't put a three-year-old on the stand, of course, but if he recognizes her, it would help me apply more pressure on her if I had a witness. She needn't know the witness is the boy."

He went on, "I think she believed that Mrs. Towerton knew something about her and that was the reason she was consulting with Mr. Prinney. Now that we have her fingerprints, we might be able to identify them on the note."

"I don't understand why she wrote the words on it wrong though," Lily said. "She was a teacher. She knew how to spell."

Walker replied, "She probably did it deliberately to focus attention away from herself to someone, anyone, less well educated."

This made more sense to Lily once he'd pointed it out.

Mrs. Prinney asked, "But why was she staying at the Gerrits' home? Why didn't she just leave the area once she'd had her revenge? Run away somewhere else, take yet another name?"

"It's my guess," Walker said, "that she knew they'd moved to California, so she was hiding there, waiting for a chance to remove the last of her belongings from Miss Jurgen's home before she permanently disappeared. She's clearly not a rational person. We probably won't ever know why she hung around. It was a stupid thing to do."

"How did she know the door was unlocked?" Robert asked.

"She didn't," Walker said. "She planned to break the lock."

Robert suddenly stood up, looking shocked, and slapped his forehead, ran out of the dining room, and galloped upstairs. He returned a moment later flourishing the key. "I suddenly remembered that I didn't want the key to get lost and I put it in that little urn on the table by the head of the stairs."

He looked very pleased with himself for a moment, then said, "Why didn't I know anything about this before? Lily, you've been hiding things from me. I thought we were a partnership."

"Robert, it just all fell together, largely by coincidence, this afternoon while you were teaching school. Did you expect me to burst into the classroom and tell you all this in front of the children?" Lily asked.

"Why not? The whole country will know about it tomorrow since Jack interviewed her today. He'll send out another of his special bulletins to every newspaper in the country."

"And my name will be in all of them," Walker said smugly, "as the arresting officer."

The next afternoon, Robert, who had forgiven Lily, said, "Let's go to the pictures tonight. There's a 'weeper' movie running you'd like. We could take Howard along if he's free. Maybe Miss Exley and Mrs. Tarkington would like it, too."

The arrangements were made. Howard Walker wasn't interested in the movie. But he liked both Lily and Mrs. Tarkington and went along to see if either of them would cry. He made sure he sat between them.

Before the movie began, Lily said to Howard, "I didn't get a chance to tell you this earlier. Mrs. Taylor told me to pass on to you that Mrs. Rennie is taking the last of the orphans into her home along with their teacher. She'll see to it that they go to good homes. And if she can't find the teacher another job, she'll keep her as a secretary and companion."

Howard said, "I knew she was a good woman. Thanks for letting me know that."

As the picture began, a beautiful young woman was walking toward the screen in a slinky white dress. Howard suddenly leaned forward to get a better look at her.

"What's wrong?" Lily whispered.

"I'd swear that's Hildy Gerrit!"

"Who?"

"By all that's holy. Yoast Gerrit was right!"

Not ready for the intrigue to end?
Turn the page for a sneak preview of the next
Grace & Favor Mystery

IT HAD TO BE YOU

from award-winning author Jill Churchill

When Lily and Robert agreed to take on a job
in an old mansion just outside of Grace and
Favor, they expected quiet, peaceful days along
the Hudson River.

Instead they stumbled into a murder investigation unlike anything the town had seen . . .

Chapter 4

Monday, March 6

As Lily and Robert were eating breakfast before going to the nursing home, Robert asked, "How many people does this Miss Twibell have as patients?"

"Only four. She has an extra room for an emergency patient and two rooms for the young nurses who help her. Two old ladies share one big room, and will talk the socks off you. One cranky old man, and one man I haven't seen except from above. He was mowing the back yard."

"If he can mow a yard, why is he a patient?"

Lily shrugged.

"How many are on the staff?"

"The two young nurses who help the patients, and change the bedding and bandages. One of them is sick, which is why Miss Twibell needs us. Apparently the two of us equal one of her," Lily said with a wry smile. "There's also a woman who lives in the basement with her child and does the laundry. And Dr. Polhemus is on call. And does routine visits."

Robert frowned. "I'm surprised she uses him. He's such an awful gossip. I'll bet the whole town knows every detail of the four patients' symptoms."

"Who else could she get locally?" Lily asked. "I don't imagine her budget allows for a full-time doctor to live there. Oh, there's also a cook and an assistant for her. I wasn't introduced so I don't know their names. Cook sent the assistant up with the trays."

"Is she a good cook?" Robert asked.

"Yes, I think so. She sent up the best chicken soup I've ever had. It also had big fat egg noodles added for everyone but Mr. Connor. He got the plain soup. There were tuna sandwiches with lots of celery and good bread as well."

"We only take that one meal, right?"

"You just had your breakfast, Robert. And I ate dinner here last night. Didn't you notice? There must be part-time local women who come in and clean everything but the hospital part of the nursing home.

"As for the patients, Miss Smith has bad hips and has to walk with sticks," Lily said. "She knows who you are and is smitten."

"I think you told me about her before."

"I probably did. I'm guessing the woman who shares her room has asthma. Mr. Connor has a broken knee that's apparently badly infected."

"Connor? Any relation to the young man Mrs. Prinney told me about who sold you all that stuff while I was gone? Oh, you must have bought those three packs of cigarettes that were on my night table from him. Thanks."

"You're welcome. The young man is Kelly Connor, Mr. Connor's grandson."

"What's Miss Twibell like? Aside from having bunions?"

"I'll let you form your own opinion. We're supposed to be there at nine."

When they arrived, Doreen had to let them in again. Lily introduced Robert to Doreen and Buddy, who was again hiding against his mother's apron, peeking at them.

"Go on up," Doreen said. "I'm told there's a problem with one of the patients which is why Betty didn't open the door," she explained to Robert.

"I step in just as there's a 'problem,' " Robert groaned quietly.

"It's not our responsibility, Robert. Don't fret," she said as they went up the stairway.

When they arrived in the living room, Mr. Connor's door was open. Mrs. Twibell was wearing her carpet slippers instead of real shoes, and standing over Mr. Connor. Betty was beside her. They were talking in low voices.

"Robert," Lily said quietly, "I'll show you where the laundry baskets are and where to take them. When we get back, I'll tackle cleaning the floors and counter and you can entertain Miss Smith and Miss Jones. That will keep both of us out from underfoot."

Apparently, this was the day that the bulk of the linens were washed. Lily took the small basket and Robert wrestled the huge one down the stairs. "They *really* need an elevator. Or one of those dumb waiters. I'll bet the Harbinger boys would know how to install it."

"I wouldn't suggest that very soon if I were you," Lily said.

They had to make three trips to get everything down to the basement.

Robert stayed in the basement to play his little radio he'd brought along. Buddy listened, too, while Doreen started the first load of washing.

Lily went upstairs and started mopping the pharmacy part of the largest room. Betty was sound asleep on one of the sofas. Miss Twibell came into the big sitting room. "I didn't even notice you were here," she said wearily. "Is your brother along today?"

"Yes. He'll be back from the basement in a few minutes. How is Mr. Connor doing?" They were both whispering so they wouldn't wake Betty.

"Badly. He always pretends he's in a coma when his wife visits. But I'm afraid it's almost true today. He's mean as a cob. I hope he at least goes gently. Betty has been monitoring his blood pressure and pulse every three hours overnight. That's why she's taking a nap."

Watching Lily wash the floor, she pulled up a chair and took off her carpet slippers and gently massaged her feet.

"I remember their wedding," she said softly. "Mr. and Mrs. Connor's. I was just a girl then and my parents took me along. Mrs. Connor was the happiest bride I'd ever seen. She couldn't stop smiling the whole time. When they turned to come down the aisle, Mr. Connor looked as if somebody had hit him with half a brick. He looked terrified at what he'd just done. She was at least a head taller than he was, and must have outweighed him by twenty pounds."

Lily smiled and started the first round of rinsing the floor.

Putting back on one carpet slipper, Miss Twibell went on, "I guess she kept track of my family. At least well enough to know I ran a nursing home. She put him in here about three months ago and visits him every week. Things have changed with them. All she does is berate him while she's here."

"What about?" Lily ventured to ask, even though it was none of her business.

"Their son Stephan and Stephan's sons. Apparently there was a big family blow up many years ago and Stephan moved to the other side of Beacon, refusing to be in touch with them and also refusing to let them see their grandsons."

"I thought you said Kelly Connor visited his

grandfather when he was in Voorburg and gave him samples?"

"Yes. But never when his grandmother is around. And he asked me to keep his visits secret from her. Which I've done. He visited this morning, in fact. He knows his grandmother doesn't come until around eleven. And the visiting nurse turned up early, too."

She sighed and donned her other carpet slipper and stood up. "Enough gossiping. I don't know what's come over me."

As she spoke, Robert came into the main room and said, "I just heard on the radio that Mayor Cermak died today."

Both Lily and Miss Twibell shushed him, pointing at Betty.

"Oh, the poor man. Having to linger like that for three weeks," Miss Twibell said quietly. "It's a shame, but good that the assassin didn't shoot our new president as he meant to."

"It was a close thing," Robert said. "Roosevelt had just given a speech and was still standing in his car. Cermak was standing on the running board."

"Miss Twibell," Lily said, "I suppose you've guessed that this is my brother Robert. He didn't give me the chance to be polite."

"I guessed," Miss Twibell said, smiling. "Now I have to get real shoes on. This is the day Mr. Connor's wife visits."

"What's up?" Robert asked when Miss Twibell had gone.

"She thinks he's going into a coma. It must be almost the end for him."

"I don't want to be around for that," Robert admitted. "It would be better to visit the two old ladies. Do you need any help?"

"No, thanks. I'm almost done. I'll tell you when the bell rings to pick up the finished laundry."

"I'll await that as eagerly as you think. Getting it down there was awful. Getting it back up will be worse. You're sure I can't mention an elevator?"

"Not today," Lily replied firmly.

Mrs. Connor arrived an hour later. She walked into her husband's room, leaving the door slightly ajar. The first thing she said was, "Don't think you're fooling me, Sean. I know you're awake. I have some farm problems we need to discuss." There was a silence, then she must have gotten up from the chair next to his bed, realizing she was being heard. She slammed the door and went back to talking. But the words were muffled.

Miss Twibell had been in her suite putting her nurse shoes on and hobbled in just in time to hear this.

Betty still sat on the sofa but sitting up, rubbing her eyes, still half asleep from being up most of the night checking on Mr. Connor. Miss Twibell sat on a chair next to the sofa, putting her feet up on the center table. They didn't speak.

Lily got busy cleaning the counter now that

she'd finished the floor, thinking vaguely that she probably should do these chores in the opposite way. Counter first, in case she dropped pieces of lint on the floor. As she finished up and was heading for the closet to put the mop away, Mrs. Connor opened the door of her husband's room and shouted, "He's not breathing!"

Betty and Miss Twibell leaped up and hurried into the room, Miss Twibell closing it behind them. Even with the door shut, Lily could hear Mrs. Connor wailing and sobbing. "I really thought he'd get better and come home and go back to work."

Miss Twibell and Betty brought Mrs. Connor out of the room and helped her to the sofa. She was still sobbing and hiccuping. Miss Twibell pushed a bell by the door and the cook's assistant showed up in a moment. "We need three cups of strong tea and sugar, please. As quickly as you can."

The girl was back in moments. Mrs. Connor's sobbing had stopped and she was mopping her eyes and nose with an oversized handkerchief with a lace border.

"What do I do now?" she asked. "How can I take care of the farm all by myself any longer? The workers don't like me. One of them walked out this morning. That's what I wanted to talk to Sean about."

"Don't worry about that now," Mrs. Twibell said. She'd been through this any number of times when patients reached the end of their lives. "First, you need to make the funeral arrangements."

"I'll bury him on our land where all my family are buried," Mrs. Connor said. "That's only right."

"You need to consult his attorney first to see if he had a will leaving instruction for his wishes," Miss Twibell told her. "Would you like me to call and make you an appointment? I also need to call Dr. Polhemus to sign the death certificate."

"Oh, I hadn't thought of that. Yes, please." Mrs. Connor told her attorney's name.

Lily went to Miss Smith's and Miss Jones's room. She really wasn't entitled to eavesdrop anymore, and didn't want to appear to be doing so.

Miss Smith was laughing uproariously at something Robert had said. Miss Jones was smiling as she was sewing two narrow strips of knitted work together with a curved blunt needle.

"What's so funny?" she asked. Miss Smith was laughing so hard she couldn't explain. Robert rose from the one chair and gestured for Lily to sit in the chair, and then said to Miss Jones, "Would it be improper if I sat on the foot of your bed?"

"Better than the floor," Miss Jones wheezed. "You'd get bits of yarn all over your trousers."

They chatted for a half hour but couldn't help hearing a trolley rolled into Mr. Connor's room and leaving a few minutes later. Lily hadn't intended to tell the pair of old ladies that Mr. Connor was dying. But they guessed when they heard the noises. "He's gone then?" Miss Jones asked.

"I think so," Lily said.

"Good riddance," Miss Smith said. "He was a nasty man. I have friends in Beacon and they told me years ago about him cheating his son."

"How?" Robert asked.

"Connor and his only son Stephan owned a rental property," Miss Smith explained, "or so my friend said. Connor wanted to sell it. The son didn't. So Connor forged his son's name on the deed and sold it anyway. And he kept all the money. His son was furious. Connor's wife took her husband's side and between them they drove the son and grandsons away. From the way we hear her talking to him these days, she must have changed her mind about his morals since then."

Robert heard a bell ring and they went to see if it was Doreen alerting him that the first load of laundry was done. It was and he went away reluctantly, muttering about elevators.

As Lily stood around at loose ends, Betty came out of Mr. Connor's former room, carrying a pillow and sheets. She took Miss Twibell aside and showed her something. Miss Twibell nodded and headed for the telephone in the main room.

"Give me Chief Walker's number please," she said to the operator. It took a few minutes for the operator to find him. He wasn't at the boardinghouse where his main office was. She finally located him at the jail.

Miss Twibell said, "Chief Walker, this is Miss Twibell. Could you do me a favor? Would you call over to the funeral home in Beacon and tell them not to do anything to the body that's on the way. We'll need an autopsy done before they embalm him. I've already told them this, but they might consider me a silly woman making something out of nothing. I'd like a chief of police, either you, or their own chief in Beacon, to back me up on this. Then come up here and see what my nurse found. Meanwhile, I'll call Dr. Polhemus to tell him not to file the death certificate yet."

"What's happened?" Chief Walker asked.

"I'd rather tell you in person. You know how those girls at the telephone exchange listen in. And I have something you need to see."

Walker had been chatting with Jack Summer when the call came through.

"I'm putting the next newspaper issue together," Jack had said. "Have you had anything I can report?"

"Nothing but two drunk drivers, one accident due to ice on a driveway back last January. And a boy putting a quarter on the railroad tracks to see if it would derail the train."

"Really boring winter for you, huh? No serious crimes to investigate since that woman bumped off the preacher in November."

"I like it when Voorburg is boring. It makes me

feel like I'm a good cop, and the citizens are mostly good people. I'm sticking with the job, even though I had some good offers from bigger cities, thanks to your reporting my arrest in a case of the murder of such a well-known person and passing it on to national newspapers."

"I had a few job offers from that case, too," Jack said. "I also turned them down. I like it here in Voorburg, too."

Howard said, "That might have a little to do with Mrs. Towerton, I suspect."

"Not that that's anybody's business, but I have been courting her from time to time. She keeps trying to pretend it isn't really courting though."

That's when the phone rang.

"What was that about?" Jack asked.

"Miss Twibell at the nursing home wants to tell me something she doesn't want the phone operators to hear."

"May I come along with you? I've already been in touch with her about doing a piece for the paper about the history of the nursing home as part of that series about the old homes on the hill above the village."

"You may come with me, Jack. But if it's serious police business, which it sounds as if it is, you can't report on it until I give you permission."

"Fair enough."